The Ups and Downs of Carl Davis III

The Ups and Downs

of Carl Davis III

by ROSA GUY

A Yearling Book

Published by
Dell Publishing
a division of
Bantam Doubleday Dell Publishing Group, Inc.
666 Fifth Avenue
New York, New York 10103

ISBN: 0-440-40744-3

Reprinted by arrangement with Delacorte Press

Printed in the United States of America

January 1993

10 9 8 7 6 5 4 3 2 1

OPM

To My Loves:

Warner (Dedier) Guy, the Third; Warner (Warnerque) Guy, the Fourth; Charles (Chief) Guy; Ontonia Guy, Ameze-Rosa Guy—and to lovely Coleen

The Ups and Downs of Carl Davis III

To Whom It May Concern:

This collection of letters taken from me to be compiled by Rosa Guy was written about my opinions on the state of the world, the state of the country, the state of my mind, when, to say the least, I was the most

CONFUSED!!!!!

Dear Mother,

In our family it has always been generally accepted that I am quite an intelligent boy. That's because, in our family, we have always regarded truth and openness as our greatest virtue. As you know, there are few things that happen in this world of which I am unaware, or on which I do not hold an opinion. Yes, I am often alone. But I am not a loner. Books and newspapers are my constant companions. And although I am often repelled by the ordinary youth of my age (and they by me), I have always been most satisfied with, have even been made happy by, the frequency with which Selena and Russell move in and out of my life.

I tip quietly around the house while you are working on your doctorate in nursing (as you always seem to be doing), or while Dad is resting, during his free time, from interning at the hospital (as he always seems to be doing). I perform willingly any request upon demand, even those I find most irksome. Unquestionably I am a most unusual child, a most respectful son.

Therefore, I regret to admit (while conceding my distaste for such an admission) being thoroughly confused. Ma, why did you and Dad send me to stay with Grandma!!!!

Why after twelve and three quarters years of happiness and unhappiness and confidence shared did your face begin to tighten like those of so many *ordinary* mothers we have known? Why did you thin your lips and stiffen your spine when you made that puzzling announcement "I am sending you down South to your grandmother"?

Mother, New York City is home. My home—and yours. This southern town where you have sent me is the place to which your husband, my father, Carl Davis the Second, can't go home again to stay. I need an explanation, but it is apparent neither you, your husband, nor his mother is willing to give one. Let me put you all on notice. I hate country life!

Your confused son,
Carl Davis the Third

4

March 3

Dear Mother,

I used to love coming down here with you and Dad summers. It was fun then. I often think about the year when Russell and Selena came with us. That summer it seemed there wasn't enough time in the world to do all we wanted before it was time to go back home.

Now time stands still. I leave school, where Grandma has registered me (and what a time to start a term in a new school!!!), do my homework, my chores, sit on the front porch, and stare out over the yard, into the forest beyond (thank God for a lovely, spacious yard), thinking, wondering, *Why? Why? Why?*

Of course, it's too soon for you to have received my letter. But when you do, respond immediately or I shall go mad! Indeed, had I been another type of child I would already be having severe emotional problems. But that would only burden Grandma. Besides, she warned—with flint in her eyes—"God don't cotton to folks what gives in to simplemindedness. Me neither!" Being an astute person I accept her at her word.

Here I sit waiting to hear your side of the story—so to speak. And, Mother, no telephone calls. I insist on getting your explanation in writing—a documentation, if you will, of your rationalizations as to why I deserve this punishment—being sent down to Spoonsboro (my God, no wonder its young rush to leave), South Carolina.

Your confused,
Carl Davis the Third

5

March 13

Dear Mother,

I'm settling down—slowly. It's hard. I hope that whatever reason you created in your mind to do away with me (that's what you did) will be the reason—now carefully reconsidered—for you to ask me to come back home.

By this time it must have occurred to you that no intelligent young man of twelve and three quarters should have things done *to* instead of *with* him—done without his knowledge and permission. I particularly resented how everyone involved (no one raised even one objection) pretended that all was as it had always been, when it was so obvious that everything had changed.

Suddenly my parents could no longer look into my eyes. Do you know I had to keep dashing to the mirror to inspect myself, assuring myself that my ears hadn't suddenly become misshapened? They kept burning from your rapid glances which kept sliding off the sides of my face.

And I did not speak! Never have I been so silent! Indeed, no one gave me the opportunity to utter one word in my own defense. Defense! Why defense?

On the train coming down I had the sudden thought: *Perhaps I'm too short for my age.* (You and Dad are so wonderfully tall.)

But, Ma, I'm still growing!

Yes, I am a bit plump. I do pick at food in the fridge and I eat too much junk food. But sending me down here surely will not help my weight problem. Did you forget Grandma's fried chicken and deep dish cobblers?

If I were to consume one quarter of these calories at home—I can hear your voice from here to eternity. . . .

I keep asking myself, is it because I looked at too many programs on television? I never did, you know. Besides, Grandma has a television set which she looks at morning, noon, and night—when she's not going to church or her church meetings. I keep her company—sometimes. I try to. But I have absolutely no patience with the level of programs she chooses.

Don't misunderstand me, Mother. I love Grandma. She is a little dull. But what can one expect from a person living in this slow southern country-town? Her greatest occupation, outside of church, is the thought-consuming programs on that stultifying tube which takes up half of her living room.

What a life to have condemned me to. If you have given this problem serious thought, Mother, you must, by this time, have started to fathom how utterly confused your actions have made me.

> Your unhappy and confused,
> Carl Davis the Third

Dear Mother,

Finally a letter. It said absolutely nothing. You're giving me a chance to adjust? Adjust to what? Learning how to behave down here in the sticks? Or perhaps adjust to the strange twist of your mind in sending me down here? To neither of which, I fear, will I ever adjust.

To offset my gloom Grandma talks about her unhappy years spent in New York City. To console (confound?) me she uses this worn cliché: "New York is a good place to visit, but only a fool would want to live there." (Me a fool!!!) Obviously she never discovered during her time in that city how many churches can be found there.

I try to explain New Yorkers to her. "They're a very active people," I say. "They work continually on social, economic, and political fronts to bring about change." Her answer is to smile and nod her head and say, "And no matter how hard they work, things up there sure don't change."

When I talk to Grandma about world problems—in Africa, the Middle East, Europe—she nods and smiles. She considers herself warning me: "Junior"—she insists on calling me Junior. I detest that—"remember one thing. Little black boys go to school to learn, not to teach." (Your mother-in-law thinks me an ordinary child!!!!) Sometimes she pats me on my head and says, "You're such a bright boy, Junior. I know you understand."

I am bright. But I don't understand! Does she think

that patting me on my head will prevent me from sharing my accumulated knowledge with my brethren at school? How dare she? (Besides, I cannot stand being patted on my head!!!)

I ache from the need to tell her the many things that I actively dislike her doing. But she's so happy having me here with her. And as I do have a fondness for the old lady, I allow her her pleasures. What to do?

Still unhappy and still confused,
Carl Davis the Third

Dear Mother,

It is nearing the end of my third week in this school, and as I had anticipated, the curriculum is backward and boring. When I tell Grandma, she only says, "Just so long as you're learning . . ."

One would have thought that you had apprised her that my intellectual ability transcends that of most children my age—and that there was a real possibility that there's nothing much to learn down here. Or perhaps you have told her and she's just playing games.

She insists on doing things for me. She picks up my clothes from the floor as though I'm too plump to bend. She washes my clothes and irons them (irons!!!), even my underwear! She sends me off to school spotless. Is she doing this to add to my confusion? To undermine my courage? She has.

I die inside at the thought of her smooth, sweet brown face, with its I-love-that-child look, losing its tenderness when (if) I say to her, *Grandma I cannot stand this nonsense. I want to go home. Now! This minute!* With courage gone I nod my head to her nod, smile back into her smile (my God, do I get tired of smiling!), when she asks if I'm happy to be with her.

For the first time in my life I'm living a lie! I'm pretending to enjoy life in the country, in her little house (I didn't remember this house as being so tiny), when the exact opposite is true.

I try to help Grandma. It doesn't work. One day I came in and there was Grandma waiting to greet me, her arms wide open. Naturally I opened my arms wide too.

(She's such a tiny, dainty lady, isn't she? How did she manage to have a son as big as Dad?) Her eyes kept getting wider, and when I put my arms around her I heard a crash. Her best vase had fallen off the sideboard, never to be the same again. Mom, I swear I don't know how it happened. I don't remember the living room being so crowded. It's a large room. But the big television takes up almost an entire wall, and the overstuffed couch and chairs (which she has had since before Dad was born), and the big coffee table and all of her doodads on them. How can one maneuver? (If not for her lovely yard—back and front—into which I can escape, I would suffocate.)

I told her I was sorry. She smiled. (Why must she smile when she had to be displeased?) "Never mind, Junior," she said. "What's done is done."

When I tried to pick up the broken glass, she stopped me. "No, no, Junior, let it be. We can't have you getting splinters in your fingers, now, can we?" (How different she is from you. You would not have smiled if your *worst* vase had been broken. Nor would you have let me up until I had picked up even unseen slivers.)

Whenever I try to help around the house, something happens. A few of those silly doodads fell off the coffee table. (Why does she need all that junk?) And one day her crystal ice bucket fell by some crazy accident. "Junior, you're so strong," she said. "Don't you think you best help-out in the yard?"

So now I rake leaves, put them in a big can, and burn them—strange how in the country leaves pile up, even in winter. Ma, did you know that burning leaves smell like pot? To stretch my work time I work the earth around Grandma's gardens—vegetable and flower. When I have finished that (orgy) I read. What else?

Bored and disgruntled,
Carl Davis the Third

Dear Mother,

I have come to the conclusion that Grandma is a very happy person. Her happiness comes from doing the most uninteresting jobs ever created. When she's not looking at TV, or going to church, she cleans house. When that's too clean to touch, she washes and starches clothes and irons. She takes special time with doilies—they are everywhere in the crowded living room: on the table beneath vases, on the end tables beneath lamps, on the backs of stuffed couch and chairs—then she cooks.

When Grandma cooks, she doesn't fool around. She hits those pots and pans in her little kitchen and things happen! She cooks for her church meetings. And on Sundays she invites some of the church members. Many of them once lived out here (before gentrification) and are glad to be able to come back to visit—and eat. She has one friend, Deacon Johnson, who comes out twice and sometimes three times a week for that pleasure.

A funny man, that Deacon Johnson. He owns a big high-powered Cadillac. He drives it right up to the front door, looking high-powered-important himself behind the wheel. Then he steps out. His knees buckle, he shuffles up to the front steps, knees bent, hands shaking. He has to grab hold of the banister to pull himself up the steps, shuffles into the house, heads for the table, and then—a miracle.

With what force that deacon pushes forkfuls of food into his mouth! "I knows you cooked this here part for me, Mary Jo," he says as he reaches for a piece of chicken (the part that goes over the fence last). And with what power he chews (grinds) the backbones to a paste with those worn brown teeth. When he finishes that piece he reaches for his next favorite piece, then his next. Deacon Johnson loves chicken!!!

After dinner Deacon Johnson shuffles out to the front porch, where he sits rocking in the old rocking chair while Grandma clears off the table.

He's not much of a talker. The first evening he asked me what I planned on being. "A doctor?" he said, nodding his head. "Fine, fine. The race will always be needing doctoring."

I agreed but told him that medicine certainly was not my preference. "I want to be a political scientist," I said. Then I told him that the actions and reactions of peoples to ever-changing world situations held the greatest interest for me.

He laughed and asked Grandma, "Mary Jo, this boy always talk this way?"

"Always did," Grandma said. "From the day he was born, seems like to me. Remember when he was two. His folks bought him a tweed suit. You should have seen him strutting, his rump sticking out—always did have a big rump. Acted then like he was about to take on the world—still does. That's the way with kids of old folks —either too dull or too bright."

Old folks! How dare she? I see you now at your desk, your ageless brown face glowing in the lamplight. And Dad, forever silent, so deep inside himself, hardly talking but his forever-young eyes laughing, crinkling at the corners. (By the way, Mother, you have never told me your exact age.) Never mind, the image of you two—

my mother, my father, like that, is deep within me. (We are a family who love each other, aren't we?????)

The old deacon said to Grandma, "Well, he talks as though he *thinks* he knows what he's talking about." I had to warn him.

"Sir," I said, "I am a very knowledgeable young man."

He laughed. "Well, that means you'll be doing all right in that school for bright kids," he said.

I told him I thought the school was adequate but that my teacher, who is also my social studies teacher, left quite a bit to be desired. That startled him.

"Now, you look here, boy," he said. "That ain't no way to talk. That teacher happens to be teaching in that school on account she knows what she's about."

"One generally supposes that about teachers. But that hasn't always been my experience, and it definitely isn't in Miss Attaway's case."

My answer triggered his bones to a sudden response. He sat up straight in that old rocker shouting, "Who do you think you are to question a teacher?"

Of course I had to tell him: "Sir, I'm Carl Davis the Third."

I actually saw a bit of foam form at the corners of his mouth! Then he became nasty. "That's what's wrong with our black folks," he said. "Always running out at the mouth when they ought to be listening. Never knows nothing and ain't never gonna learn nothing." Driving around in a big Cadillac certainly had done nothing to boost his self-image. Of course I disagreed. "You must remember, Deacon, how recently blacks were granted, by law, the right to attend integrated schools in the South—or even sit at counters to eat. Now a black man has run for president. Isn't that astonishing—when one considers how slowly history turns?"

Mother, he turned on me. "Talking about that fool Jackson," he said, "what if he had been voted into office? What would have happened? Well, I'll tell you, the country would go to the dogs, that's what. Just look at them Africans. Look what done happen over there since the white man left and Africans taken over."

"Deacon," I said, "we might or might not be talking about two different things here. But let us assume we are talking about the same thing.

"First, if you're saying that had Jackson won the presidency, he might never have been allowed to govern by those truly in power, I agree. Second, the whites never left Africa.

"We know the Western powers had no intention of letting the wealthiest continent in the world out of their grasping hands. So when they knew independence was imminent in their African colonies, they gave to them so-called independence in order to maintain control through puppets.

"You do remember Patrice Lumumba? When the Belgians gave independence to the Belgian Congo, they chose Patrice Lumumba as their boy. When they discovered that to Lumumba independence was more than just a dream word, they killed him and replaced him with someone more to their liking. Sir, let us now discuss the question of neocolonialism. . . ."

He snored. Ma, you know how I delight in a fruitful

discussion. But in the middle of my talk Deacon Johnson had fallen asleep!

Poor Grandma. Before I came, all she had to keep her company evenings was her television set and that old feeble man. What a miserable existence.

Which makes me understand the responsibility I have to her (making my stay here even more depressing). But never fear, Mother dear, Dad's mother's life shall be interesting as long as I'm here.

> Your devoted and responsible son,
> Carl Davis the Third

Dear Mother,

From your letter dated March seventeenth, telling me, of all things, that I must listen to Grandma (who else???). My God, what evasion! Have you come to the point where you are unable to answer direct questions with direct answers and telling me to pay attention in school! It appears that I have not conveyed how exceedingly difficult it is for me down here. Not only because of my insoluble confusion about my parents, but the school I must attend—and my teacher!!!

Most of my teachers (and I say this in all modesty)—English, math, and language—have accommodated themselves to me—to my brilliance—and I to them. But with my homeroom teacher—who, as I said before, happens to be my instructor in social studies—it was obviously hate at first contact. Our chemistry, to say the least, reacts most violently when we are in mutual proximity.

On my first day at school I tried to be polite, correct, helpful, all those traits that make my personality grand —providing, that is, I'm not abused. (I do feel strongly that I am being abused by you and Dad.) I smiled when I met her, bowed. "Anything you want of me, Miss Attaway," I said, "feel free to command." Her answer? "Sit down!" Since that day that's all I have been doing.

Miss Attaway is of medium height—obviously an old maiden. Her lips are pursed, she wears her gray hair pulled back in a bun—which, I presume, might be responsible for the stiffness of her neck, the unbending quality of her back. Her eyes are a slate-blue—or gray—

which reflects (pardon the disrespect) a most limited intelligence.

To be more gracious: Miss Attaway's interpretation of history leaves much to be desired. Of black history she knows little and I hazard a guess that she cares less. In other words, it's safe to assume that Miss Attaway and I view history from different perspectives.

She speaks glowingly of Jefferson Davis and harshly of Abraham Lincoln. She regards the defeat of General Custer as a great American tragedy, and describes the American Indians as mere savages (still!!). Her idea of black history is that it is an adjunct of European history, starting with the Middle Passage and ending with our enslavement. So what about our most recent past? Our current status? And who are we black kids sitting in her class? Aberrations?

If I needed proof of her state of mind (which I didn't), I overheard her speaking with my math teacher on the stairs: "Brilliant?" I heard her say. "The only thing brilliant a black can do is polish silver—and shoes." My math teacher said, "I hope you give the new boy, Carl Davis, a chance. He's the brightest kid in his grade." To which Miss Attaway said, and I quote: "Carl Davis? That arrogant, fat little beast? He sits in class like a frog waiting for a princess to touch him—to show off his brilliance. I will not be the one to oblige." A princess? Ha!

Yes, Mother, you sent me here and so deserve the mental anguish you are now experiencing. But never fear, Mother dear. The days are gone when a highly motivated, knowledgeable black student might have been tarred and feathered because he had the audacity to differ with a white teacher (a practice which my august parents succeeded in abolishing).

And so I sit dutifully in class and listen to all Miss Attaway's drivel. Never do I volunteer, therefore I never am in a position to disagree. From time to time, however, when she makes a particularly asinine statement, her eyes are drawn to mine. I allow her to read my thoughts. She quickly swivels her head away. It's safe to assume that Miss Attaway has real problems about including me in classwork.

The students sense her hostility toward me and react to it: the whites regard me with equal hostility, the blacks with shame. It's a fact, Mother, the black kids refuse to look directly at me!

Once in a while (to hear the sound of my voice) I direct a question to the teacher. Then her back stiffens. She pretends not to hear. But a general restlessness races around the room—a shuffling of feet and of paper, giggles—which I must say is most disconcerting. I hate to be ignored and I hate being laughed at!

This high school has only recently been integrated. One year! (After all this time!!!) The students are carefully chosen for brightness. So the tenth-grade students are younger than the average. They don't possess that Terrifying Energy (TE) which marks the adolescent. The white students are carefully bright. The black students (there are five in my class—three boys including me and two girls) are bright. But bright! All spit-and-polish shining shoes, glowing faces, white shirts or blouses, ties —really. . . .

There are twenty black students in the entire school and only those in their senior year wear sweatshirts and sneaks. I think it's because hairs have started growing on their chins. That Terrifying Energy—that's what gives them confidence.

Blacks and whites in their senior year seem to get along, obviously because of their sharpening intelligence. The boys going to this school are not as threatening as those whites (pregentrification backwoods) around the same age who simply hang around the school waiting for a chance (an excuse?) to mix it up with their more learned brethren. Those boys have nothing but TE working for them. They don't go to school, nor do they work. Around the school they make eyes at the girls and wait for the schoolboys to challenge them. Down here I can't make myself invisible as I did in New York. It's easy for the toughs to spot me. But at least I'm short for my age. (The things that I have to be grateful for!!!) They go after big guys.

But back to my class: The black students are most attentive. They sit, listen, nod their heads, and grin when Miss Attaway, unable to avoid their wildly waving hands, condescends to call on them. Their struggle (yes, I conceive it as a struggle) to be recognized as smart is obscene—downright obsequious. Never do they challenge Miss Attaway. The questions they ask, the answers, are taken from the social studies books given us (to learn!!!!).

Don't misunderstand me, Mother. The schools in New York are not much different. There, too, students get passing grades for studying the miserable dated books. But at least in Special Classes, *we are special.* We are graded for alertness, not for nodding and grinning. We are encouraged to disagree, to debate, to discuss—not simply to accept. In other words we are invited *to share* a learning experience.

I try to explain this to Grandma. She scratches the top of her blue head (yes, Grandma dyes her gray hair blue) and warns: "Junior, you go to that school to learn, not to make a nuisance of yourself." Grandma expects me to be ordinary! I am not an ordinary child!

There's a boy in class—a black boy, Reggie Owens (does Dad know any Owenses down here?), a tall, good-looking boy with intelligent eyes. There are times when, after Miss Attaway says something I find particularly offensive, we exchange glances. He averts his eyes, ashamed. Yet I feel we share similar views. One day I approached him, but his friend, a tall, red-haired gangling boy, pulled him away.

When school is over the black kids rush to get to their buses for the ride back into town. The white students? It's safe to assume that their friendships were cemented at the beginning of the school year or before. Those who live in the vicinity of the school haven't broken ranks to admit this black boy. I'm not complaining. I am accustomed to being alone. Now I am in a new town, a new school, with my old habit—being by myself. (It feels like loneliness down here.)

There is a girl who lives out our way. Inge Anderson. She lives in a new luxury (gentrified) house. Inge's family comes from Sweden. Her father works for the United States government—a secret project. No one knows for sure, so Mr. Anderson's suspected of being an under-cover agent, a double agent, a spy, or worse. Deliver me from provincial towns.

I haven't seen Inge's father. Only her mother and brother. They're a family of look-alikes: platinum-blond, fair skin, clear blue eyes. Her mother's tiny and her brother tall, broad, with an unhappy air—TE re-strained? (Is there such a thing as restrained adoles-cence???)

Inge is weird. We walk along the same lane going home, sit in the same classes, yet she never looks at me. She did, at first, and I thought we were getting along— until the day I said, "Inge, you ought to wear your dresses longer." Giving her good advice, Ma.

"How dare you look at my legs?" She accused me! I told her that I never looked at her legs but other boys did.

Mother, she wears party dresses to school—short— and her legs are fat! She wears knee socks, baby-doll shoes, and ribbons in her hair. She must be at least thir-teen! She looks out of place and I told her so. Since then she sticks her head up in the air whenever I'm around. She talks to those boys who look at her legs and snicker when she's out of hearing.

The girls like her. They swarm around her like bees, complimenting her, touching her hair, her clothes. Miss Attaway, too, has made her a favorite. And when she walks down our lane (always in front of me), she preens!

I find her attitude totally reprehensible. How impos-sible to cultivate the friendship of a person with such vanity. I had hoped we might be friends, the way I was with Selena. But then, Selena and I grew up together. We were brother and sister—almost. . . .

Speaking of Selena, how is she? You said you had seen her but didn't tell me exactly what she was doing. And Russell? I didn't have time to contact him before leaving. I will write to him soon. But until then I would appreciate it if you . . . No, Mother, I beg you, please call him, tell him I'm sorry I hadn't the time to say good-bye. Russ is my best friend, Ma. And you ought to have let me talk to him before you sent me off. I love him—really love him—and miss him. . . .

Your still bewildered,
Carl Davis the Third

Dear Mother,

I have heard you say that there are days when the atmosphere is in such a state of turbulence that everyone is affected (full moon?). Today was such a day. In class today my attention had wandered. Of what was I thinking? Of you? Dad? Russ? In these days of confusion many things occupy my mind. Through a haze I heard my name.

"Carl Davis—I-am-speaking-to-you!"

My mind snapped back. My head snapped up. I found myself staring into the evilest I-got-you-now smirk. Miss Attaway had called on me, in a most underhanded manner. A betrayal of the highest order. We had had a pact of sorts—I thought. Silence had been our status quo: Don't-you-talk-to-me-and-I-won't-talk-to-you. I see now she had only been waiting!

And she had chosen her time well, to touch this frog. I stretched my imagination to see her as a princess. But no. Only a pinched-faced hag in a gray dress stood there, a malicious smile in her slate-gray eyes, with a contemptuous *V*-for-victory smile turning up her cruel, thin lips—which of course sharpened my resolve to do my princely best.

Being the student I am, I knew that subconsciously I must have heard all that had happened in that room.

On the blackboard the name Christopher Columbus and the year 1492 had been written. Impossible for this special class to be into such elementary history. I concluded it had to be history in review. So I rambled about things that were little known about Columbus: his adventures before setting out to this hemisphere; the influence of the Prophet Esdras on his thinking that the world was round—an opinion he later discarded, coming to the conclusion that the world was pear shaped; that he was Italian by birth, but might have been of Jewish-Spanish ancestry, his father having moved to Genoa some time before his birth.

As I spoke I studied Miss Attaway's face for a sign that I might have touched on her question. From the intense pleasure it reflected, I knew I hadn't. Also, the restless shuffling of feet, the rustling of papers, the slamming down of books on desks, reinforced that conclusion. Then I heard a boy say, "That bag of wind ought to sit down." And another: "Let's stick a pin in him and blow him down." And when Miss Attaway said with glee, "Sit down, Carl Davis," I had no other recourse but to open a head-on, wide-open discussion.

"It is claimed that Columbus discovered a new world," I said. "Utter nonsense. This hemisphere is as old as Europe and was peopled when Columbus first landed. But Columbus, in his arrogance, believed that he was the first to have discovered a 'new world' and a new people.

"The island which he called San Salvador had been known before him as Guanahaní. Savages, he chose to call the inhabitants, and he condemned their religion because they were not Christians and claimed their lands for himself and the Spanish crown."

I smiled. But Miss Attaway's eyes had narrowed to slits. "Sit down, Carl Davis," she said. "You have been waiting for a chance to prove your brilliance. Let me inform you this attempt has proven a failure."

The kids snickered. It didn't matter. Whether they knew it or not, *I had broadened their knowledge.* Whatever questions had been actually asked I considered irrelevant.

"Many of these gentle peoples," I said, "showed to Columbus and his men great hospitality. But he soon lost their confidence when he forcibly removed seven of them from Guanahaní. Then they believed all Spaniards to be like the cannibals of the Carib tribe who came up the coasts, from lands to the south, to capture and eat them.

"They were not wrong in thinking that the Spaniards were dangerous. As governor of the lands he had explored, Columbus made his brother Bartolomeo administrator, and Bartolomeo forcibly removed most of the occupants of Guanahaní for work in the mines of Hispaniola, leaving San Salvador depopulated.

"Columbus always had colonization and slavery on his mind. In his notes on the Arawaks, who inhabited the island of Hispaniola, he wrote of their 'intelligence, industry, and handsomeness—a people who would be good to be *ordered* and made to work, sow, and do all necessary to adopt our ways. . . .'

"Indeed, on his second voyage Columbus came with clergy, additional men, and all tools necessary in the development of the colony.

"It's true that in the establishment of the colony the aborigines often rebelled against their captivity. It's also true that grave dissension among Spaniards occurred—

due to Columbus's poor administrative skills and his obsession to find the land where "gold is born." This forced the monarchs to issue a decree preventing him from returning to his precious Hispaniola. But there is a far greater truth: The colonies had been established, Christianity had been introduced, and in the years that followed, forced labor, murder, rape, bloodhounds, diseases, artificial famine—the destruction of crops to starve those who rebelled—all but annihilated the Arawaks within one generation! This situation so anguished the Dominican priest Las Casas, that he beseeched the Spanish government to repeal laws of compulsory labor and begged that the stronger black men, from Africa, be sent to replace the natives.

"In 1517—eleven years after Columbus died, twelve years after his fourth and last voyage to this hemisphere, twenty-five years after he first landed in the "New World"—the first fifteen thousand black men were brought from Africa, and chattel slavery began in this hemisphere—and that over one hundred years *before the Mayflower*!"

Mother, I was absolutely brilliant! I wiped the smirk from Miss Attaway's face, halted the restless shuffling of feet. "Carl Davis," she said, "I asked you to sit down! You have chosen to ignore me. I want you to report to the principal's office this instant!" I went. The principal wasn't there. She refused to let me back in class. So I sat in his office until the bell.

Now for the second incident of this turbulent day:

Upon leaving school I saw Reggie Owens and Ted Thompson rushing to catch their bus. I wanted to talk to them, to get their view of my presentation—or as one might say, at least have them give me A for effort.

Before I got to them, two white toughs stopped them. "Hey, nigger," one said, "we been looking at you trying to get close to our white gals."

"Look, man," Reggie said, "we don't want no trouble with you."

Whereupon the other tough said, "Hear that boy, Jeb? He don't want no trouble. Then what he doing looking at them gals?"

Jeb is thickset with pimples over his face (TE stinking out of him). He's not taller than Reggie, just bigger and older.

When I saw what was about to happen I ducked back into school. (Ma, you know how I abhor violence.) I rushed to the office, told the clerk. She called the sheriff. I kept peering out the door, seeing how the boys were pushing Reggie and Thompson around, trying to goad them into fighting. When I heard the police sirens I pushed my way through the crowd. "You had better stop," I warned them. "I heard the names you called these boys. I saw you shoving them around. I hope you understand the seriousness of your act. . . ."

"Look at the little blimp," Jeb said, grabbing me by the jacket. "I'm gonna close that big mouth but good."

I had timed it perfectly. The sheriff came through the crowd right behind me. The toughs let me go and ran. I grinned at Reggie, thinking he would be pleased. Instead he snarled. "You sure a smart-ass," he said. "You Negroes from up North gives me a pain in my ass."

(Negroes! Where has this young man been!) "Your'll come down here and make things bad for us."

"It seems to me, Reggie Owens, that those two toughs were the ones making things bad for you," I said.

"We can take care of them," Reggie said. (How, by rattling to death?) "You didn't have to come on with that damn big talk and all that slavery crap in class today."

"In class?" I was surprised. He had just been almost beaten up and all he had on his mind was the lesson in class.

"That crap about Columbus," he said.

"Crap? You call history crap?"

"You call that stuff you were talking, history?" he said. "If you keep your big mouth shut, that would be history.

"You know how long it took us to be admitted into this school?" he said. "A long time. And we don't want no up-North city smarts coming down here making things rough on us."

Mother, I had just saved this boy's life! Yet he appeared to be more upset about my upsetting Miss Attaway.

"Reggie Owens," I said, "my name is Carl Davis the Third. I gave you credit for a bit of intelligence. My error. The only aptitude you seem to have is the ability to bow so that your head can touch a white person's feet. We, up North, call that Uncle Tomism."

He jumped at me. (Jumped me!!!) Thompson got between us and pulled him away. No, I would never fight him. He's six feet tall!

Now for the third upsetting incident:

By this time it was quite late. Certainly too late for Inge Anderson to be still around. Yet as I started walking down the lane, there she was in front of me. She looked over her shoulder at me, up and down, then pushed her head up in the air and walked on—switching.

God, how angry that made me. (Why does she always have to be walking in front of me switching without talking!!!!) It also made me sad. I thought of Grandma saying to the deacon that I was one of a kind, and Deacon answering, "We sure got a lot to thank God for." Yes, I am a difficult child.

But in New York at least I have you and Dad. And Russ and Selena, who accept me as being difficult, and can still love me. I don't want to sound as though I'm begging—I am. I want to come home. Please let me come home. Whatever I did that made you send me here, I'm sorry for. Tell me what and I promise I won't do it again. I miss you. I miss you all so very, very much. . . .

Tomorrow is another day. Let us hope the atmospheric disturbances which affected everyone today have subsided. I wouldn't want to have a meeting with the principal, Mr. Adamson, under such tumultuous circumstances. At any rate things can't be much worse. Yesterday I thought I had the possibility of a friend. Today that possibility has become an improbability. Tomorrow? We'll have to wait to see what happens tomorrow.

> Your troubled and lonely son,
> Carl Davis the Third

Ma,

Today I made a friend.

Did I tell you that I go fishing in the woods? I do afternoons after school before I do my homework. I made a fishing rod, which I keep in the trunk of that hollow tree beneath which Dad sits to do his fishing. Sometimes I catch a "mess" of catfish. Catfish are always so hungry, they bite at everything. I have learned to clean them and Grandma fries them. Grandma loves catfish.

Well, there I sat, my back to the tree, my line in the water, when I heard a bark and this dog came running to me. He jumped on me, licking my face. One would have thought he had known me forever. I, too, felt that I had known him in another place at another time.

Weird coming from me? But I suppose being lonely makes believers of us all. I call him Spots. He's a white bull terrier and has a black patch around one eye.

What a wonderful time we had. We rolled over the grass. I took a stick and threw it into the lake. Spots dived in. He swam out and brought it back to me. A retriever!!!

I took him home. But Grandma wouldn't let me keep him. "Found?" she said. "Junior, how can you 'found' a dog when he has a collar around his neck?"

I hadn't seen it. I guess I hadn't wanted to see it. I told her that whoever owned him couldn't be very nice because he had adopted *me*. Grandma refused to listen. "Take him back where you found him. I don't want no trouble with these folks around here."

Grandma is always concerned about getting into trouble with "these folks," meaning our white neighbors. Then why does she live all the way out here? She's the last black person, except for Farmer Whitley, living around these parts. The rest moved out because of gentrification. Most of her old friends sold their homes to wealthy whites. They all live in town. Grandma goes to town to church and to visit, but as she tells it, she has no intention of selling or being run off her land. She claims she intends to die and be buried here on this land which she and her husband bought and where her child was born. She claims she left it once (going to live in New York) and she'll never leave it again. I agree with her. Still, if she did move, I might have someone to play with. Perhaps even another Russell.

However, now I have Spots. I want him. When Grandma insisted I take him back to the lake, he followed me home again. No matter how much I begged him, he refused to leave me. Then Grandma put her hands to her hips, looked at him in his eyes, and said, "Listen, dog, I don't want no trouble outta you. Go on home now. Git!" She pointed to the road and Spots put his tail between his legs, rolled his eyes at her, and trotted off. He turned back to look at me, but Grandma still stood there pointing. So he kept on going. What a smart dog! And it doesn't matter he was forced to go, I shall see him tomorrow. It's so wonderful to have a friend, Ma.

                              Your loving son,
                              Carl Davis the Third

P.S. I went to the principal yesterday morning. He's okay. Soft spoken. I like him. He listened to us patiently, then asked Miss Attaway, "Did the young man ever answer your question?"

"No," Miss Attaway said. "I had asked who was the first European to land on the North American mainland. Carl Davis stood up and rambled on about Columbus, refusing to be silent, or to sit when asked."

Embarrassed!!! When the floor didn't open up to receive me, I sought total recall. I had the feeling (knowledge?) that Miss Attaway, knowing I had not been listening, was now twisting the lesson to her advantage. But whom to ask?

"Well, Carl," Mr. Adamson said, "can you answer the question? Who was the first European to land on the North American mainland?"

Leif Eriksson? But he had merely stumbled on the landmass with no intention of exploring it. "Ponce de León . . . ?" I murmured, praying. How upsetting not to be able to think clearly.

"And the year?" Mr. Adamson kept up, fueling my embarrassment. I stammered. (Can you imagine me stammering!!!) He nodded, smiling, forgiving me my confusion (something which I would never!). "I'm sure, now that we have had this talk, things will go more smoothly in the future. Carl will be more attentive, won't you, Carl?"

I nodded. What else? Not until his door had closed behind us did the year 1513 pop into my head. I wanted to shout it out to her loud enough for him to hear

through his closed door. But by that time Miss Attaway
had walked away from me, her *V*-for-victory smile over
me set onto her face—fait accompli. And I? I have to sit
in her class and watch her gloat!!!!

April 1

Dear Mother,

I found Spots's owner. Or rather she found me. Guess who it is. Inge Anderson, the Swedish girl in my class whom I detest.

Spots and I had been meeting every day for over a week. We love each other. I never had a dog (you always talked about getting me one. Why didn't you ever?) and so I never knew how close a dog can be to this boy.

There we were sitting on the bank of the lake, peacefully fishing, when I heard this screech: "What are you doing with my dog?"

"He's my dog." Pure reaction. I feel that he's mine.

"You stole him," Inge accused me, and realizing my mistake I retracted—immediately. "I didn't steal him. I didn't mean he's mine," I said. "I meant he's always here —with me."

She put her hands on her fat hips and said, "So, that's where he is when I'm looking for him? I don't want you to play with him anymore."

That, of course, is impossible. To demonstrate the impossibility I threw a stick far out into the lake. Spots leapt up, dived into the water, and swam out after it. All the while he swam, Inge kept shouting, "You come back here. Do you hear me?"

He never listened, which made her furious. When he came out of the water, she grabbed his collar and tried to pull him away. But Spots had to give the stick to *me*. When she tried to take the stick from him, he growled deep in his throat. That frightened Inge and she let go of the stick. But instead of taking the stick away from

Spots, I held it in his mouth while she kept shouting, "Let him go. Let him go."

"Do you see me holding him?" I asked her.

"Yes, you are holding him," she said. "Look at him. He's cold—shivering from being in that water. I'm going to tell my brother on you."

Spots was wet, but he wasn't shivering, nor was he cold. I let go the stick and said, "Spots, go home." Spots trotted off. When Inge saw how he listened to me, her face got ten shades of red, her clear blue eyes flashed lightning at me.

"How do you know his name?" she asked.

"I named him," I told her.

"Liar!" she screamed at me. "You're telling lies. I named him Spots."

When I heard that, I knew that Spots may be her property but in his heart he belongs to me. So I laughed, trying to be friendly. After all he was, like it or not, our dog. "He told me his name," I joked.

"You're always trying to be so smart," she said. "But you're retarded. All the kids in class know you're retarded. The teacher knows you're retarded."

That angered me. I shouted back, "You have a fat ass." She has. She's plump. Her legs are thick and she has a dimple right in a roll of fat that laps over her knee-length socks.

"You're not thin," she said. "Your behind sticks out when you walk."

"At least I wear pants," I answered. "Nobody can see my underwear. But every time you bend, everyone looks right up your dress. They see your underwear and your fat ass!"

That, I must admit, Mother, was not Carl Davis the Third at his intellectual best. But never had I been that angry.

And she? She kept shouting. "I hate you, Carl Davis. I hate you. I'll be glad when Miss Attaway gets you out of our class and sends you where you belong—a school for the retarded!"

Tears came to her eyes and she ran. I didn't care. How dared she call me names? I hate ignorance. And Inge Anderson is as ignorant as the rest of that class. As stupid as Miss Attaway.

I have to pass her house on the way home. She lives in a big house—the first on the road from the lake. And when I walked by, I heard her saying in a loud voice, "Spots, you never must play with that retarded boy again. Look how wet you are."

I whistled. Spots barked. I knew she had to be holding him, or he would have come. I whistled again. Spots yelped. She had hit him! I wanted to go right then and take him away. But her door opened and I heard this male voice. It might have been her brother. I ran home. After all, he is about eighteen with a lot of TE. . . .

Mother, my life has become even more complicated. Now I love a dog that belongs to someone else—someone I hate. I really hate Inge Anderson.

Your son,
Carl Davis the Third

Dear Mother,

I certainly am glad that I wrote telling you of that terrible girl Inge. Her mother, Mrs. Anderson, came to see Grandma to complain about me. I was on the front porch when she came so I heard her, in the yard, telling Grandma that I was not a good boy, and that I had said unkind things to her Inge. "He made her cry," she said.

Grandma called me to defend myself. "Junior, what did you say to Miss Anderson's little girl that might have upset her?" she asked.

Knowing how careful Grandma is about getting into trouble with her neighbors, and not wanting her to hear what I had said to Inge, when I was playing with her dog, I tried not to tell. "I didn't call her anything as bad as she called me."

"Then you did call her names?" Grandma asked.

"No," I said. "I just told her she was fat."

"Ooooh," Grandma said. "*You*—call someone fat?"

But Mrs. Anderson had not finished. "Not only that, but he tried to steal her dog."

Thankfully Grandma was in on that from the first. "Now, that's not true, Mrs. Anderson," she said. "That dog followed Junior home. I had to chase him away."

I like Mrs. Anderson. She is very pretty—and slim. Her accent is nice—so different from the southern drawl. But then she said sympathetically to Grandma, "I know how it is, Mrs. Davis. He's retarded and you feel you must take up for him. But he must be careful what he says to others."

That puzzled Grandma. "My grandson retarded?" she said.

"I hate to be one to complain," Mrs. Anderson said, "but please, try to control him. My Inge is so sensitive and he's always bothering her."

"That's a lie!" I was so angry I shouted. "You're a liar, and so is your daughter."

I have only spoken to that girl twice. Worse, I hated seeing Grandma just stand and listen when someone calls me retarded.

"Junior," Grandma said, "you don't talk to grown folks like that. Whatever Mrs. Anderson has to say, we can discuss. But I will not have you being disrespectful. You must apologize."

"I shall not," I said. "No one calls me retarded and gets away with it. Mrs. Anderson, I happen to be a very astute young man. Far more than your daughter, or any of her classmates. I am the closest person to a genius that your daughter will ever have the good fortune to meet. Good day." I walked away from her.

Just think—I actually liked Mrs. Anderson. I dislike her now, as much as I do her daughter. I shall not, no, I shall never, listen to insults heaped upon me and be forced to apologize besides.

Your indignant son,
Carl Davis the Third

Hi, Moms,

Things are getting much better down here. True, Grandma is still giving me the silent treatment. She doesn't forgive me for not apologizing to Mrs. Anderson —something that, of course, I shall never do. Inge holds her head higher and walks stiffer when she walks by me. For my part, I never look her way.

Since seeing the principal I have changed my behavior. I sit in class and never look at Miss Attaway. She ignores me. Reggie, who I once thought might be a friend, is now my sworn enemy. He glares at me, waiting, I believe, for a reason to slam into me. Needless to say I have no intention of giving him such an opportunity.

I sit in class and listen to all that is said (respectfully) even when I disagree. I read the terrible books, take the simple tests—and pass.

Then the bell rings and I rush out of school, down to the woods, where I know Spots will be waiting, or soon will come. How wonderful to have a bright spot in my life, never failing me. It's so wonderful to have a dog. One that loves me and can tell me in so many ways without words.

Why did I never have a dog in New York? Didn't you trust me? To think, almost thirteen years—almost to that time when my TE will take me and swirl me into another dimension—without ever having a creature so wonderful. . . .

Your son,
Carl Davis the Third

Hi, Mom,

I met Johan, Inge's look-alike brother. But they are not that much alike after all. I had been afraid to meet him after all those charges and countercharges between families. But he turned out to be a wonderful fellow. Today he came to the lake while I was fishing. Spots sat beside me but Johan didn't mind. He only smiled.

I like his smile. A real heart-to-eyes smile (know what I mean?). Johan is seventeen and, boy, does he have TE. Sitting near him one can sense his restlessness, inside. He's good-looking. Girls would find him so. Tall, with the broad shoulders and wide chest that they go for. I never saw him with a girl.

Spots likes him much more than he likes Inge. I told him Spots was a retriever. He hadn't known. We threw sticks in the water for Spots to retrieve as we talked.

Johan hates this town as much as I do. "Everybody wants you to do what they do," he said. "Everybody wants you to think as they think."

"Which would be all right if they did interesting things or thought interesting thoughts—or even intelligent thoughts, even if they weren't interesting."

"Exactly." He agreed with me, and we looked at each other, liking each other. Yet he felt the difference in our years more than I did.

"I miss my father," he said.

"What does your father do?" I asked him.

"He works for government," he said. "Secret. We don't discuss. When he took the work he brought us here to be near him. But we still don't see him too much."

I thought of Dad and how much I long for him—and for you. "I like you," he said. "My sister, my mother . . ." He tapped his head and laughed.

I wanted him to stay and talk to me. I wanted to let him know that despite my size—and boyish look—I wasn't so young. "Why don't you stay and fish?" I said. "I catch some big fish here."

He shook his head no. "This lake is too small," he said. "Back home I go fishing on a big boat in the ocean. You must come to Sweden when I go back. It is not so big as this country. But then, the city where we live is not so small as this town."

He walked off toward the woods. I kept looking at him until he disappeared in the thickness of trees. He reminded me, suddenly, of Russell. He, like Russ, must have outgrown his friends. Johan is white and Russell is black. Yet they are both of a type.

I think that boys who are big for their age sometimes feel like strangers to themselves—especially when they're not close to their dad. Their height, their broad shoulders, make them exciting to girls. They react to the excitement. I think it makes them feel grown. But they're not always ready for it. They want to give in to the excitement, yet it frightens them. They become confused, restless. TE.

Selena and I used to worry about Russell. Ma, did you know that Selena was my girl until Russ got so big and handsome? Then she fell for him. I don't hold it against her. After all, she's always been more like my sister—really.

Seeing Johan go into the woods, all by himself, I felt his loneliness surround me, the way Russ's loneliness surrounded me. I know how deep that loneliness can be. So I said to Spots, "Go with Johan!" And that intelligent dog sped off after him. The longer I know that dog, the more I love him—really love him, Ma. . . .

Inge was sitting on the front porch as I walked by going home. She seemed disappointed not to have to squint her eyes and give Spots hell for following me. Strange girl, that Inge. Real strange girl.

Your loving son,
Carl Davis the Third

P.S. I haven't heard from Selena or Russ. Have you seen them? I dropped Selena a line, but she hasn't answered. If you see her—them—please tell them to write, to call—do something. . . .

Dearest Mother,

Yesterday while raking the yard, I heard a bird sing. I looked up at the birdhouse (Grandma keeps one at the side of the house) and saw a cardinal. Never have I seen such a beautiful creature. The cardinal is the most perfect bird—tiny, a round head, and unbelievably scarlet. Grandma said it was a male. Female cardinals, she said, are not so lovely. It doesn't matter. That such loveliness exists anywhere in this world is a miracle.

I have now become a bird-watcher—a most satisfying experience! In New York the only birds that call attention to themselves are the sparrows—and, of course, pigeons. Other birds visit the bird sanctuaries, I know, but I have never seen them and so had never been interested in bird-watching before.

What a spectacle of colors! What differences in forms! In habits! Blue jays, blackbirds, woodpeckers—to name but a few.

My next step naturally became animal watching. Here, too, there are a variety: chipmunks, raccoons, hares, opossums, skunks. How wonderful.

Do you remember how, when you explained to us—Russ, Selena, and me—about birds and bees? How we giggled, nudging each other. We knew you were trying, in your gentle way, to teach us what we had already learned on the streets, at its most vulgar—sex.

Living down here, observing these animals and birds, one is constantly aware of sex and is delighted by it. How wonderful that this act—which had kept us nudging and leering, in a most repulsive manner—continues the reproduction of these species of exquisite animals and spectacular birds, like the cardinal.

There is a charm about Grandma's house being the first on the lane leading down to the lake and woods. I love walking down that lane. The trees on both sides make every home private—private estates. I get a Huck Finn or Tom Sawyer feeling strolling alone, never seeing anyone. All the occupants of the houses are so invisible, they might as well be absent, and I have the world to myself.

I listen to the birds in the woods, hear animals scurrying in the underbrush, and reprimand myself for having ignored all of this wonder during our summers down here.

What fun if Russell were here with me. Russ and I often went to Central Park. We fished in the ponds seeded with little fish by the Parks Department for our pleasure.

The memory of those days is with me constantly as I take giant steps between sunshine and shadow on the road to the woods, or as I race down the grassy slope to the lake where great big fish are waiting to be caught.

Do you remember Farmer Whitley? He still lives in the backwoods—the last of the black farmers who once occupied land around here. Daddy will remember him. He remembers Dad. I met him down by the lake. What a wonderful old man, Farmer Whitley. He still rides a mule cart in the forest to collect dry wood. (He burns wood to heat water.)

"Once long ago," he said, "fish in the lake were so plentiful that all a fellow had to do was stand on the bank, a line and tackle in his hand. Fish would jump out of the water begging, 'Catch me, catch me.' " Farmer Whitley is funny—sometimes.

Then he tells about the other farmers who once lived here and how they were run off their farms to make room for the luxury estates. Farmer Whitley refused to sell and the builders tried to scare him out.

"I was scared," he said. "Them crackers can be scary folks. Downright evil." He was so frightened that many nights he didn't sleep in the house, he slept in the woods instead. "And just like I known it would happen, it happened. Woke up one night and my house was just a-blazing. Burned right down to the ground before these very eyes, it did. But you see me still here, don'tcha?"

Farmer Whitley has two sons living in Atlanta— lawyers. "Ain't raised them with my years of hard work for them to be sitting in big-time cities, being big time to big-time money folks, while I gets burned out," he said.

He sent for his sons and they came. They took the case to court and Farmer Whitley won. He got the money to rebuild his house. "Ain't had no running water till then. And I got me a good inside toilet now too." Then he said, "Still remembers the time that couldn't happen. Time was when white folks say move, you moved. Or you find yourself swinging from a tree—like that there gal Billie Holiday used to sing. Like some strange fruit." He shook his head. "But that time's gone. That President Johnson done changed things for black folks down here."

I tried to remind Farmer Whitley that the laws had changed because black folks had fought, and some white folks too. I spoke to him of the freedom rides which you and Dad took part in and of the mobs that overturned and burned buses with freedom riders, of how Dad and other young students were beaten and tortured.

Farmer Whitley listened, nodding his head. He scratched his chin and chuckled. "Yet," he said, "that President Johnson—don't let nobody tell you different, boy. That was the greatest president what ever lived."

There're a lot of Vietnam vets who might disagree. And knowing how you and Dad had been a part of that movement that had forced the change which he was giving President Johnson all the credit for—indeed, having spent my entire life being proud of your participation in it—I feel somehow that you were being written out of history. Not only by white historians but by black folks who gained the most from your struggles. I guess the memory of black folks isn't any longer than that of whites. But it should be, shouldn't it, Mom?

Things haven't changed—completely. We might not be swinging like "strange fruit" from the trees, but when I feel the tension in the way whites look at blacks (especially the tough boys with all that TE), I wonder.

It's a subject no one down here discusses. Sometimes when I'm with Johan, I know we think about it. We start to talk, then something happens and our eyes slide past each other. We change the subject. It should be talked out. There seems a danger in not talking it out. . . .

However, right now I'm enjoying life. I wait most impatiently for the end of a school day to walk down to the lake, to be soothed by soft winds, and maybe get a chance to see and talk to Johan or Farmer Whitley, or just to be calm and patient waiting for fish to bite, or to bird- and animal-watch with my devoted Spots.

If you and Dad and Russ and Selena were here, as in bygone days, life for me would be perfect. I love you and miss you all.

Your loving son,
Carl Davis the Third

April 18

Dear Mother,

A strange and terrifying thing happened to me, which I can't get out of my mind. I had sent Spots into the woods searching for Johan. When he didn't come back I went in search of him. At first I didn't find him and was about to give up when I heard his bark, walked in the direction from where the bark came, and found myself at a clearing in the woods which I had never seen. Someone's hopped-up wreck was parked in the clearing. As I approached I was struck by the scent of burning weeds. I saw in the distance smoke rising from Farmer Whitley's place and supposed at first the smell had to be coming from there.

But it was more present, more persistent, and so I kept my distance from the car, although Spots stood barking, welcoming me. The strangest sensation invaded me: When one smells burning weeds in the city, one knows somehow that it's pot. In the country one expects to see *leaves* burning. I had the distinct feeling of being in two places at the same time. In the car were boys. But what would country kids be doing smoking weeds?

The faces of the boys, when they turned and saw me, became still—as death, to use a cliché. Their faces froze into blankness, their eyes grew stony, hostile. Mother, for the first time in my life I felt my skin prickle with the threat of imminent death.

I remembered the talks we had about students being tortured by whites, of whites putting out burning cigarettes on young naked black flesh. I stood staring, unable to move. These boys were white, and older, strong with TE—seventeen, eighteen, perhaps even nineteen. The thought flashed that out there in the woods I was helpless. I stood still, staring, the way a rat must when hypnotized by a snake.

Then one boy—whose back had been turned—looked around. Johan. He laughed when he saw me, got out of the car, put his arm around my shoulder, and walked me out of the woods. The smile he gave as he left was apologetic. I wanted to call after him, tell him to stay with me. I wanted to keep him with me. I never said a word. I watched his back disappearing through the trees, with that same strange feeling of being two places at once. I had played this scene before. . . .

At any rate, Ma, Johan really saved my life—I think. Isn't that wild!!!!

> Your truly confused son,
> Carl Davis the Third

P.S. Ma, how free are we? How quickly can we lose our individuality? Our confidence? Our freedom? Our life . . . ? It strikes me. Lovely woods can hold great danger—men.

Dear Mother,

I received your (short) letter dated April sixteenth. I have been writing long, impassioned letters to you and have been receiving notes instructing me to behave myself and that you and Dad love me. Let me state beforehand, at length, my shock at your reactions, the conclusion you have reached based on my many letters.

Yes, I understand you and Dad are both hardworking. Yes, I know you haven't had much time with me. You never have had. But that you sent me down here because you know I love it??? My dear Mother, I believe that you have been led to think me as retarded as Miss Attaway and my classmates claim.

No, I am not sulking in school because I'm peeved. No, it's not my intention to get even (with you?). No, that is not why my teacher and I are not getting along. And I must inform you that I do my homework—well—before going fishing and playing with Spots. The situation in school is exactly as I described. My problems with my teacher stem from the reasons I have stated.

I am not being arrogant, as you implied. When I first came to class I was exceedingly polite. Our difficulty did not arise from the conversation I overheard between Miss Attaway and my math teacher. I merely mentioned that to you, to underline my difficulties.

When on my first day in class Miss Attaway informed me that she was also my social studies teacher, I was delighted and told her so. "I am exceedingly interested in how one, in the South, conducts seminars on the life and times of such a great leader as the Reverend

Martin Luther King," I said. She stared, looked around (to see who was listening, I guess), then asked, "Who?" looking down at me as though I *were* a toad.

An insolent woman. Perhaps it's because she's so old. At any rate her demeanor suggested ignorance, or contempt, of modern American history. Nevertheless I continued with charm. I joked. "Never mind, Miss Attaway, you need not fear, Carl Davis is now here—and is most knowledgeable on that subject."

Her answer? "Sit down!"

Yet you, hundreds of miles away, presume that you can second-guess *my conduct*! How dare you go through the many letters I have wrung from my heart and pick those you think best describe my behavior? How dare you question my motives? How dare you show more sympathy for an unsympathetic teacher whom you cannot know, than for your own unhappy, confused child!!!

The love that you profess to hold seems strangely lacking. Perhaps it always was. Perhaps, unable to continue your thirteen-year deception, you had to bundle me up and ship me off to your husband's mother.

Indeed, with such a revelation it's quite possible that I shall develop incurable emotional problems—even if Grandma doesn't allow them.

No, no, you have no need for concern. Now that I understand the true nature of our relationship, I have lost all desire to return home to New York. I have reconciled myself to an indefinite stay with Grandma—and Spots.

> Your dismayed and disillusioned,
> Carl Davis the Third

April 27

Hi, Dad,

I haven't written home for some time. I do so now only to tell you that Grandma's arthritis acted up today. She sent me to town to do her shopping. A great experience. I stepped from the bus and one of Grandma's church friends recognized me and introduced me to another old friend of the family. Before I got to the market, I was introduced to several friends who had known you as a boy, who had known Grandpa when he was a boy, who remembered the day Grandpa and Grandma were married.

Many thought I looked like you. One man said you had been short and fat as a child. You, Dad? Short? Fat? Then maybe I still have a chance. By the way, I have pushed up a bit—almost five five now.

Many of those I met had been old neighbors of Grandma's in the country. Some thought Grandma had been a "mite" too proud. They said she ought to have taken the money the white folks offered and moved to town. It's important, they said, for folks to stay together.

I enjoyed meeting them. They promised a picnic or a party where I can meet kids my age. (Kids my age!!! How I detest them!!!)

On my way back on the bus I thought of New York and of Russ. We used to leave the apartment, take a bus to Central Park, travel those miles without ever seeing a grown-up who knew us or whom we knew.

We spent hours in the park fishing in the pond beneath the Castle Belvedere. After that we climbed the

54

hill to the castle and stood looking over the fields (the fields where we picnicked while waiting to get tickets for Shakespeare in the Park), where boys from private schools play soccer or football. Their cries reached us but we never could distinguish one word from another, except the word no. That word travels far.

On the way home on the bus not one grown-up ever looked at us, even when we bragged, at the top of our voices, each trying to convince the other (and anyone who would listen) who had caught the biggest of those small fish.

Russell needs to be in a place like this. A town where people knew his father and grandfather. Somewhere where he belongs. Do you know how it made me feel, Dad? Like I had an arm around my shoulders.

I have written to Russ. I have also asked Mother to write to let me know what's been happening with him. Apparently she has her reasons for not responding. I'll write to him again. But if you see him, please tell him he must answer.

> Your obedient son,
> Carl Davis the Third

P.S. By the way, Dad, I believe Grandma is sicker than she makes out. When I came back from town she had been in bed. She rushed to get up when she heard me. I know she did, because neat-as-a-pin Grandma had put her housedress on on the wrong side. And her bed was unmade! I pretended not to notice. But Grandma!!!

Even when her arthritis acts up, she can't stand an un-made bed!!

Deacon Johnson had stopped by. After I had been back for a while, he came shuffling out of the bathroom, knees all stiff and bent. Guess he thought he would surprise Grandma into hustling those pots and pans . . . ha-ha, joke's on him.

I certainly am glad to be here with Grandma now that I realize that she's ill. Just think how awful it would be if the only one she had to depend on was old rickety-bones, when her arthritis starts acting up.

April 27

Dear Russ,

What's been happening, man? I wrote to you and you haven't answered. I ask about you but evidently no one has seen you. I miss you. There's no one down here I can talk to or have fun with.

Do you remember the time we all came down together? You and I and Selena jumped into the lake naked. Remember how we kept pushing Selena's head underwater and how she fought to get away? And when she got out how she took our clothes with her so we had to walk home naked? It seems that we were so young then—I mean young. . . .

There's a girl down here we could really upset, man. The way we used to upset Selena. Remember how we would get her book bag and change her homework so that when she started to read in class, she would ape out? And the time we taped up her skirt in the back so that when she switched trying to put us down, folks looking at her from behind saw her panties? . . . ha-ha. No, we certainly were not always nice guys. But we sure had fun—until you decided that you were in love. . . .

This girl Inge we could drive crazy. She tries to act stuck up the way Selena used to. Man, we could have so much fun. Down here there are snakes and worms and things . . . ha-ha. . . .

Russ, please write to me. I miss you and want to know what's happening with you.

Your best friend,
Carl Davis the Third

Hey, Russ,

In trying to decide why my folks got rid of me, I think of two incidents—of which I'm sure they know absolutely nothing—unless you told them at a much later date.

The first: the time I cut school to go to the hospital with you. You had a bitter taste in your mouth and said your gall bladder was leaking. Remember?

We were sitting in the emergency room of the hospital when some boys came in, beat up and bruised. They had been in a rumble. Suddenly police were swarming in. They picked up all the kids in emergency who were there without parents. A boy had been shot in the rumble.

They pulled us in too. No one listened when we tried to explain. Then they started fingerprinting and we refused to be fingerprinted or to give our names. The police asked the other boys who we were. The boys looked at us and said, "Who they? Man, how we supposed to know? We don't keep a list on dudes you pigs drag in." They let us go then.

I never told Mom. It's a delicate thing changing the inner workings of one's mind. My mother's image of me was of a boy—good, if talkative—sitting in school challenging teachers, not sitting in jail reading my rights to the police.

The second incident: the time boys jumped us in the park. Tough teenaged school dropouts, heavy with TE (strange how dropouts of that certain age, black or white, give out the same signals—trouble). They were pushing you around, when I tried to talk them out of it. I got a black eye for my troubles. (I told Mom I'd walked into a door.) They chased us and we jumped into the lake and wouldn't get out until the police came and chased them away. We dried our clothes on the old pipes in my basement, remember?

That was a day of great decision for me. If I told the folks what had happened, they might say I had no right to be hanging out with older kids. That was always Mother's fear—the difference in our age. I keep wondering about that time—did she find out . . . ?

Well I'm here—a fait accompli. Grandma is getting on in years and really needs me, so the possibility exists that we may not see each other again—unless you can make it down for a visit. So let's keep in touch until that time—shall we, Russ? So please let me hear from you. Please. Please. . . .

> Your truest, trusted friend,
> Carl Davis the Third

P.S. By the way, Russ, whatever happened to your gall bladder? Did those cops scare it out of you? Ha-ha. I never heard you mention it again.

Dear Dad,

Grandma's friend gave a party in town so that I could meet kids my age. As you know, kids my age are invariably much younger than I. And these kids are even younger than those my age in New York. Everyone sat around staring at me. I might have been an alien from outer space.

There was one girl, however, somewhat older—about fifteen, sixteen—who pretended a lack of interest except when she wasn't noticed. Then she would whisper, "I want to go to New York one day." The southern accent, when it comes from the lips of a pretty girl, is enchanting—particularly when it gives out that dreamy quality. It made me feel the great guy from the greater-than-life big city. I asked her name. She blushed and mumbled so that I never caught it.

She gave me ice cream and when I began to eat, she watched every spoonful as it went into my mouth and down my throat. I really felt *the celebrity*. If only she had had the courage to speak to me when everyone was looking.

All in all I'm glad that Grandma refused to give up her place in the country. Her house is not so small after all, and we do have the wide-open outdoors. These town apartments are small, the streets are narrow, the traffic heavy—pollution at any price. Another inner city has been created. How imprisoning to be in that crowded room staring back at staring faces. But to go outside, where the older boys hung out, is another story.

Ted Thompson, Reggie's friend, is the grandson of

one of Grandma's friends. He came in (obviously he preferred outside to in), saw me, whispered to his grandmother, and left. I suppose he told her I was a troublemaker. Because later all of the elders thought it their duty to warn me.

"You best be careful down here, son," one said. "Things ain't like they be in New York. In South Carolina we still watch our step." Then another: "You and Thompson sure is lucky to be in that school for bright childrens. You mustn't make it bad for one another."

"Perhaps I am lucky," I said, "but so are the other children in my class. I was admitted because of my mind —and I guess Ted Thompson was too." Why is it that *we* always have to be the ones to be so thankful, Dad? The other kids are equally blessed to have us around.

"I'm being very careful in school," I told them. (I am, Dad. I haven't uttered one word in class since my tragic embarrassment.) "I wouldn't do anything to ruin Thompson's or Reggie Owens's chances," I said. "I just wish that they would teach the class black history."

Whereupon an older gentleman said, "Black history? What in the hell is black history, son?" (Shades of Deacon Johnson!)

"I mean the history of black folks," I said, getting up to take my leave. It was getting dark. The pretty girl had the courtesy to appear disappointed. As to the rest . . .

No, Dad, I'm not arrogant. Just bored.

Your son,
Carl Davis the Third

May 10

Dear Dad,

Are you surprised by my sudden need to be heard by you? For years (ever since I can remember), when I have had a serious discussion, or a vital point to make, you have answered me with grunts, raised eyebrows, or an acknowledging wink. Why do I expect a change of character? I don't, really. However, now that the closeness I had shared with Mother no longer exists, and since Grandma doesn't understand me, I am reaching out to you—for a wink, I suppose.

You must have read my letters to Mother and so already know that my teacher Miss Attaway and I are not chemically attuned. I had made it a point to sit quietly while I'm in her class and just listen—protecting her, so to speak, by my silence. Why did I break my silence? Perhaps I was bored.

Miss Attaway had asked the girl sitting directly in front of me to state the gains brought about by the Revolutionary War. The girl answered, "It gave to the thirteen colonies independence from Great Britain."

"Correct," Miss Attaway said. "But the word *revolution* itself, doesn't it mean total change?"

I found myself on my feet answering. "The war which gave us our independence in 1776 merely set the stage for a continuing revolution," I said. "A revolution which reached a high plateau with the Civil War in 1861 and an even higher plateau when Rosa Parks stood up for her rights by sitting in a bus in Montgomery, Alabama, a move which precipitated the civil rights struggle of the nineteen sixties and seventies in which Martin Luther King took a leading role."

Whereupon Reggie Owens stood up to challenge me (challenge me!!!!). "The Revolutionary War did mean total change, Miss Attaway," he said. "The Declaration of Independence gave to each man, for the first time, inalienable rights which all men were bound to respect. They include life, liberty, and the pursuit of happiness."

"What about the slaves?" I asked him. "Were they not men? Didn't the framers of the Constitution have slaves? Didn't Washington? Didn't Thomas Jefferson have slaves? Were the slaves freed?" I asked. Whereupon Miss Attaway turned to me, let her eyes go over me from head to foot, and with an ugly smirk stretching her face, said, "Obviously."

"The slaves were freed by the Emancipation Proclamation in 1863," Reggie Owens said, sounding bright. But bright!!!! While the slur passed way over his head.

The other kids heard. And such a snickering. Such a shuffling of feet. My cheeks, my ears, just burned. I sat down in utter misery.

Dad, I think it was the first time (despite all my rhetoric) that I felt overwhelmed. Crushed. To have such a thin strip of history to even mention, in the vast sea of history of the States, and to have that strip overlooked, ignored, washed away. It wipes one out, doesn't it?

I was upset enough to go to Mr. Adamson after class to explain what had happened. "I tried very hard to take part in class," I told him. "And Miss Attaway rewarded me with a racist slur, sir."

"Perhaps you misunderstood her," he said after I

had explained. "At any rate I will have a talk with her. Miss Attaway is an excellent teacher—a firm traditionalist. . . ."

"Perhaps, but we do have different interpretations of history, sir," I said.

"But she's the teacher," he said. Almost the exact words Grandma had used.

Dad, Mr. Adamson is a lovely man—big, warm, with wide hands that can cradle a head, a football, a basketball. He stood towering over me, smiling. "Can we agree that the Revolutionary War gave the colonies independence? We won it. It changed the life of man—fundamentally."

I wanted to debate the point, discuss the economic change brought about by slavery—the Industrial Revolution, which manifested itself in the Age of Revolution in France and here. How the French Declaration of the Rights of Man and of the Citizen played a most profound role in influencing our Constitution. But how with a principal who refused to see that the fabric of which he spoke might very well be flawed? And if in trying to point it out a teacher decided to squeeze meaning out of me?

I think of the horrors which you and Mother experienced during the civil rights marches, the freedom rides —all a part of our history. I remember how my hair stood on end in the woods at the threat of those boys with Johan. How shall they ever understand? How can we Americans live together as a people if those like Mr. Adamson will not (cannot?) discuss the true state of the union, and if I am forced to sit in class and listen to the racial slurs of a bigoted teacher?

"Carl, if you will only cooperate," Mr. Adamson said, "I'm sure you'll find Miss Attaway a teacher well worth listening to." He waited for an answer; then, mistaking my silence for agreement, said, "Good. We can wait for your theorizing when you're in college. The important thing now is to get passing grades. You can do it. You're an exceedingly bright boy."

Can you imagine, Dad, I must wait to get to college!!! But Martin Luther King wrote about why we can't wait. . . .

Your confused and very angry son,
Carl Davis the Third

Dad,

I haven't been able to sleep or think since I talked to you last night. Russ dead? My best friend in the world, gone? From an overdose of drugs? I shall never see him again? Life gets more and more confusing.

Suddenly I hate New York. Part of my love for that city is (was?) based on its great expectations. The expectation of turning any corner and of seeing a friend—Russ, Selena, you, Mom—made a day in New York a wonderful thing. To walk up any street, knowing that Russ will not be on any corner, would be walking with ghosts, wading into a past not fully lived—how stunning the thought.

Yes, I did suspect and kept my suspicions from you, from Ma. He smoked cigarettes openly. He occasionally smoked pot. But I didn't *want* to believe he had gone into hard stuff. We—Russ and I—always talked about "that's-the-last-thing-in-the-world. . . ."

I was wrong to remain silent about my suspicions. I accept full blame for his death. I'm guilty. I ought to have gone to Mother or to you. (I never thought of doing either.) There was always the question of wanting me to be with boys my age. She thought Russ too old. Honestly, Dad, I thought that, if my suspicions proved correct, I could handle it. Russ loved me and listened to me. But I was sent away from the city. What to do? What to do?

> Your pained and grieving son,
> Carl

Mother, Dad,

I know all. Grandma told me (unwittingly). In attempting to console me in my grief over Russ, she said, "That Russell was a fine boy. I remember that time he came down with you—he and that other child, Selena. You two were the devils together. But Russell was a right fine child. Polite. I remember him in the doorway talking while I washed dishes. He wanted to be some dentist or doctor. And he sure looked after you—and that gal Selena. Shame he had to die," she said. "See how lucky you are? But for the good sense of your father and mother you might be dead too." She spoke as though my best friend's death were a vindication! "They sure knew what they were doing, getting you out of that city and sending you down here to me."

A shock! You sent me down here to get (keep) me away from drugs!!!

But you knew I wouldn't—couldn't! Malcolm X has always been my hero! His autobiography has always been like a bible to me. He preached against the use of drugs. We talked about it. How dare you, Mother, Dad, think of such a thing?

I have been going over my every move to try to understand how I raised such a suspicion. I traced my day-by-day development from birth. Impossible! I could never have given such an erroneous impression. Then I knew! Selena.

I'm not asking. I know. I recall the day I went looking for Russ and found him in his hallway smoking with two of his new friends. One of the boys offered me a drag. I had choices: to leave immediately; to stay and act indignant; or to pretend to take a drag to upset Russ. Russ liked being my big brother. He did all things but refused to allow me the same privilege.

I decided to anger and shame Russ into not smoking, or hanging with those boys, whom he actually didn't care for. The boys had just passed me the stick of pot when in walked Selena.

I see her now, big eyes getting bigger. I see her backing away from us, then turning and going out the door —in a hurry. It isn't without reason that Russ and I always have called Selena blabbermouth. She ran right to you, didn't she? I don't hold it against her. If I had done the same thing when I suspected Russ of going into hard drugs, he might still be alive.

But how you disappoint me. How could you, Ma, Dad, accept bigmouthed Selena's word without ever once consulting me? Your action presumed that I am an ordinary child. Yet you know that I am the extremely intelligent and responsible son of Mr. and Mrs. Carl Davis the Second.

We had such a great relationship. We discussed everything—or was it only my imagination, as, Mother, you have already made clear? I keep asking myself who betrayed whom? To fully probe that mystery I have put myself on total recall. Once again I shall retrace my life from the day of my birth to the present—and then we shall discuss this subject again.

Your deeply distressed, bereaved, confused,
Carl Davis the Third

Dear Selena,

I received your letter telling me of Russ's death two days after Dad had called to tell me about it. I had been vexed with you for not writing—and even more when I realized that you may have been responsible for the rift with my parents which caused them to send me down here. By your own admission you have confirmed what I already knew. You are happy that I'm down here even though you bear the burden of grief alone? No, you're not alone. I am grieving too. You loved Russell. So did I. There was so much about him to love. He was fifteen yet gentle—much gentler than most boys his age.

There was a sweet sadness about Russ which touched me. I see the same quality of sadness in a boy I know here—a Swedish boy named Johan. Johan is seventeen. I like him. There is this remarkable resemblance to Russ around his eyes—although his are blue and Russ's brown, and although he came from all the way across the ocean. He makes me want to reach deep inside and pull out his soul to stroke.

No, Selena, I never resented Russ because you liked him. I was glad it was Russ and not some other guy. Sure, we used to hug and kiss when we were younger (I was eight and you ten), but Russ was older. I had dreams of hugging and kissing you long after you two were seeing each other. We guys are like that. (I dream of hugging and kissing girls still. But these girls down here are not to be believed.) Anyhow, you outgrew me (so quickly) and became my big sister.

Seeing you and Russ together—tall, lean, with all

that TE working between you—was exciting to watch. Strange how your energy pushed you in one direction while Russ's pushed him in another. Do you think it was because of Russ not having a dad? Was it because he was adventurous (something I have never been), thinking he could do all things with and for all people, without having to pay the price? Interesting. I must study up on that.

I am so grateful that you finally wrote to me. Please keep writing. And remember that I shall be grieving for Russ along with you—and that shall be forever.

Your brother. Your friend,
Carl Davis the Third

Dear Mother,

I have no intention of coming home as you suggested to me and to Grandma on the telephone last night. Why the hysteria? Since I have been here, you've written the most vaguely worded letters. I know you prefer the telephone. It's so much easier to change a subject. Now, however, we both know (and I resent) the reason for your past evasiveness: lack of trust. Yours for me.

Many things have happened since I last wrote to you. But Grandma and I shall have everything under control. Surely you must know that things happen (in South Carolina too) to people which do not happen to animals of any other species. I know. I observe the animals in the woods closely.

To still your anxieties I am writing to bring you up on all that has been happening. Some of which I heard Grandma trying to convey to you last night. I'm sure she'll call you tomorrow to explain when she knows (understands?) more fully.

Let me say in advance, I accept the blame for my last altercation with Miss Attaway. For homework she had given us the choice of writing a composition on a historical person whom we thought to be the greatest personality of the twentieth century, i.e., a hero. Given my grief over Russ's death, one would suppose that what happened was inevitable.

We are the greatest country in the world, the center of power. Our dynamism had to create the greatest men of the twentieth century. I thought of writing about

Lindbergh, of Thomas Edison (I have so many heroes). Then I thought, Franklin Roosevelt? Dr. W.E.B. Du Bois? But as a child born out of struggles which resulted in your having Carl Davis the Third so late in life, I decided on Malcolm X. He epitomized, for me, the struggle of black American youth. Besides, I owed something to the memory of Russell.

Again, Mother, let me point out that since your brief letter accusing me of being a troublemaker, I sit in class as the Vegetable (except for that one instance of challenging Reggie Owens). Having been so clearly "defined" by Miss Attaway, I have lost all desire to participate in class. So it's safe to say I wrote my composition for my pleasure, not intending to read it to anyone.

So Miss Attaway called on me. (Mr. Adamson called her an excellent teacher. She's at least a most negatively perceptive teacher.) I had no choice but to read.

I wrote about Malcolm X (né Little), detailing his orphaned childhood. How like the majority of black American children he had had limited educational opportunities which, in his youth, closed off job opportunities but opened up to him a life of crime: theft, burglary, then the use and sale of drugs, which inevitably led to prison.

I read of how, in prison, he was introduced to the teachings of the Honorable Elijah Muhammad, head of the Nation of Islam—a black nationalist religion. Encouraged to study, Malcolm took a dictionary and learned every word, from *A* to *Z*. This feat developed his ability as a speaker. And upon his release, after a short apprenticeship, Malcolm was made a minister in the Nation.

His first act as minister, I explained, was to discard his "slave name" Little, given by a "slave master," and adopt the letter *X*, which best expressed his orphanhood, and the orphanhood of his people, who had never known their ancestors—having been stolen and brought to this land.

Minister Malcolm X preached against the ills of a society which supported racism created by that slave past—a system which kept black youth imprisoned in ghettoes, uneducated, unemployed, directionless, easy prey to the "white devils" who poured poisons into black communities, getting wealthy on the lives of black folks.

Malcolm believed, I said, that the only way to prevent total annihilation of blacks was for blacks to practice total abstinence from all forms of drugs—including alcohol and cigarettes—and to join the Nation of Islam.

His was the voice directionless youth had been awaiting, I said. His following grew rapidly—throughout the cities, the country, throughout the world—enabling him to travel widely.

On his voyage to Mecca, the holy shrine of Muslims, Malcolm X was astonished to see and intermingle with white Muslims of many countries. In speaking to them he came to realize that all whites were not devils; that when he had spoken of "white devils," he had rather been speaking of a system which had held most of the world's peoples in slavery—sacrificing the majority for the wealth and well-being of a few. Drugs, he came to realize, were but one part of this cruel system.

It was a new awareness. An awareness which caused a strain to develop between himself and the Honorable Elijah Muhammad. Not too long after his return Malcolm X was assassinated. Today his death is still a mystery. The man who pulled the trigger was caught. But the question remains—was this new awareness responsible for his murder?

A brilliant paper, Mother. I knew it. While I read, not one paper rustled, not a foot shuffled. Then I looked at Miss Attaway. Her eyes were blazing. She was actually bristling.

"How dare you?" she fumed. "How dare you try to influence these students by writing about the life of a drug addict—a rapist?"

That made me furious, Mother. "Malcolm X was no rapist," I shouted. "How dare *you*? Because he was black? Malcolm's final break with Elijah Muhammad came about because he learned about Muhammad's exploitation of women!"

She didn't hear me. (Perhaps we have stopped hearing each other.) "I have spent this entire term trying to teach history," she screamed. The veins pushed out of her skinny neck. "I have taught this class about men significant in changing the course of human events. And you dare to take up our time with a paper on a hoodlum!"

I walked out, Mother. If I had continued in her room listening to her tirade against Malcolm X, I might have been forced to inform her about the true rapists—those responsible for the variety of colors of black Americans. I know how unacceptable that would be—to you, to Grandma, to Mr. Adamson. . . .

I should have gone right home. Instead I waited for Reggie and Ted. I really wanted to feel that at least one person was to some degree in my corner. But when Reggie came out, he charged right into me. "Carl Davis the Third," he sneered, "we guys have just about had it with you."

"With me?" I asked, puzzled.

"Yes, you. Writing about a damn junkie. Trying to make him into some kind of hero. I never heard of him."

Reggie had written about Thomas Edison (another one of my heroes. Four students had written about Edison.) "Why didn't you write about Thurgood Marshall, or Dr. Du Bois?" I asked him. "Everybody knows about Edison. Students have a right to know about black heroes. They helped make the twentieth century great too."

"Who are they?" he jeered. "If you know about them, they either got to be slaves or junkies."

I refused to tolerate such a level of ignorance, and I told him so. *Whop.* I never saw his fist coming. A million pinpoint balloons burst inside my head, blinding me. I opened my eyes to find myself on the ground, with Reggie on top of me, beating a rhythm on my face as though it were a drum. I refused to cry out. I prayed for someone, anyone, to get the ten hundred pounds of bones off me. Someone did. Mr. Adamson.

He marched us into school and made us wait outside his office while he sent for Miss Attaway. And when she came, she walked into his office, pretending she didn't see us. I knew that I was in trouble.

I sat trying to listen to hear the lies she was making up to tell Mr. Adamson. And all the while Reggie, sitting beside me, was plea-bargaining. "Carl," he said, "don't tell Mr. Adamson the reason we were fighting, he'll laugh at us. He'll say we're ignorant and that they ought never to have accepted kids from deprived areas into this school." Which was most unsettling to me. It proved that Reggie knew all about Malcolm and, instead of supporting me, had sold me out!

He had to be crazy mad, Mother. There I sat, eyes blackened, mouth fat and getting fatter, threatened with the loss of family and home (I had decided that I would leave home before I'd ever sit in that teacher's class again!!!) because this boy was ashamed and had resorted to violence to prove my great work unworthy. Yet here he sat begging me!

"Please, Carl, promise you won't tell."

"Reggie Owens," I said, "I have demonstrated my talents to the best of my ability. If the teacher and the principal will not accept the obvious, that's their loss."

I have never seen anybody as upset as Reggie Owens at that moment—sweating, whining, big round eyes begging. It pained me to see this handsome (Reggie Owens is very handsome) boy beg because of an ass of a teacher who ought to have the highest regard for him if for nothing more than his subservience. I half promised. You know—a shrug, perhaps a nod. . . .

Then Mr. Adamson called us in and Reggie had an extreme case of diarrhea of the mouth. "Carl is always after us Negro guys," he said. "He's racist and tries to make us see things—racist things—his way. When we don't he gets mad. Today he jumped me."

Surprise showed on all our faces. Even Miss Attaway had never accused me of racism. And, too, it's obvious that I'm not physically or emotionally a violent person. However, Miss Attaway did nothing to erase the stigma.

"You see, Mr. Adamson," she said. "It's impossible to tolerate this boy in my class."

Having promised Reggie—if only by a nod—I stilled my urge to blurt out the truth and cause him embarrassment. Instead I decided to take the high road. (You know: I would not so dearly love myself had I not loved honor more.) Miss Attaway's acceptance of Reggie's accusation had decided me: never was I going to sit in her room again. Never, indeed, did I intend to go back to the school. So, with great effort, I twisted my swollen lips in what I hoped resembled a sneer and gazed with blackened eyes from shifty-eyed Reggie Owens to tight-faced Miss Attaway, pleased to remain silent.

"Carl," Mr. Adamson said—he really is a fine, sensitive man—"these complaints have gone far enough. I must ask you to bring your grandmother the next time you come to school."

My grandmother! Ha-ha. If they held their breath they would drop dead. By the time they realized that that was a never-never option, and called the house, I would have decided on where I intended to make my new home and probably would be long gone. . . .

Mom, I must stop now. Grandma has just called me

in for dinner. By the way, I stopped racing Deacon Johnson to the table for my favorite pieces of chicken. It shows.

To continue: Mother, you can see why I didn't tell Grandma. All the reasons have already been stated: First, Grandma had warned me from my first day, she would tolerate no nonsense. Second, my task down here, as I see it, is to aid Grandma, not add to her misery. Third, I shall not have Grandma going to school to explain my conduct or to justify my great intellect to a Miss Attaway (both being outside the scope of her comprehension). And fourth and far from least, I shall have no one attempting to make me feel inferior because they do not agree with my thinking, nor shall I permit anyone to instill within me self-doubt.

I hear your inquiring mind: *Where is his sense of guilt?* I have no guilt! It was not my idea to be sent down here to attend a school where I'm constantly being bombarded by blasts of bigotry. Furthermore, I miss nothing by not going; my teacher has no use for my opinions and Grandma is absolutely adamant that I refrain from giving them.

So, until I have decided just where I shall spend the next few years of my adolescence, I have decided to learn something meaningful—something for which I have never given myself the time: recreation.

Mother, it is great. Mornings after Inge has gone to school I walk past her house and whistle. Out comes Spots. May I backtrack here for a spot of humor?

On the day of the fight Inge had waited around the

school until I left Mr. Adamson's office. We were walking toward the lane when she called to me. "Carl, if you tell me more about Malcolm X, I'll let you play with Spots," she said.

Mother, my face was swollen, my nose spreading over my face, my eyes half closed. I leered at her. "If you want to know about Malcolm X," I said, "do it the old-fashioned way. Read his autobiography." Indeed, why need I put up with such sarcasm? Spots is mine just for a whistle.

To continue: Spots and I roamed the woods and played. What a delightful time. We rolled on the ground, played retrieve at the lake, we bird- and animal-watched.

Perfect weather. The winds down here are sweet, warm. They glide over the skin—what luxury. (Do you know the delicious feel of air touching the skin?) Every day is too short. I even learned to tell time from the direction of the sun streaming through the trees (which is more than I learned the entire time I was in school) and so know exactly what time to start back home.

And, Mother, I discovered something startling. I have never been happy before. I have never been free before. I see my entire life now as time spent preparing my mind for combat. I have lived under siege, in a state of constant readiness against society, the enemy. Now I'm just a boy with his dog. Spots is intelligent, understanding, and has more spirit than the students at school. He laughs when I laugh (truly). He loves me and I love him. If only my freedom could go on forever.

But then, Grandma found out.

On my fourth day of liberty Spots and I were down by the lake when Johan came by. It was late morning. "Inge is not out of school today," he said.

"I know," I said.

"You're out because of the paper you read," he said.

"How did you know?"

"Inge," he said, touching his head, and we laughed.

"Is your school closed today?" I asked. He shook his head no. He sighed and we looked at each other sympathetically. Once again I thought of Russ. He looked at my still-swollen face. "You had a big fight," he said. I nodded. "Because of the paper you wrote." I nodded. "You know you'll have this fight with the boy?" I shook my head. "With the teacher?" I nodded. I wanted to talk about my last day of combat. But that would sound too glib—because he reminded me so much of Russ.

Can you imagine, this big blond Swede, from all the way across the sea, reminding me of brown-skinned, curly-haired black American Russ?

"Then why did you write it?" he asked. I told him: "All black leaders die," I said. "They are murdered and soon forgotten. Malcolm X died in 1965. One might say we are still living in his time—certainly things that are happening now were happening when he lived. Yet those for whom he gave his life have forgotten. I don't want people to forget him."

"Perhaps I'll read about him," Johan said.

"I have his book—his autobiography," I said. "I'll lend it to you."

"Okay," he said. Then he touched the blackened area around my eyes, felt the swelling of my nose. "But from now on you write—don't fight," he joked. Then he left us to go on into the woods.

Spots and I stayed at the bank of the lake fishing for some time. But I kept thinking of Johan, the closeness we seemed to feel for each other. I wanted to be with him. So I got up to go and look for him.

Spots and I were walking in the direction of the clearing when, looking up, I saw a flower growing high on the branch of a tree. It was a vivid orange. Its wide-open petals caught a shaft of sunlight, making it glow—like gold. To get a better look I decided to climb the tree.

I have never climbed a tree. But the full-limbed tree offered me no difficulty. On the branch beneath the flower I reached up. As I did I heard a ripping sound, and the limb on which I was standing began to bend, bend, bend. Then it tore—lengthwise. I fell. In falling I braced myself to hit the ground head first. Instead I found myself hanging face downward, arms and legs dangling. The branch in splitting had in some impossible way torn right through to my underwear at the seat, its jagged edge going beneath my belt to come out in the back of my shirt, its point resting somewhere just between my shoulder blades. And there I hung like a bird ready to take off but unable to flap my wings. Any attempt to reach my arms back to extricate myself from this most ridiculous position, and the jagged point, sharp as a razor, jabbed into my back, while my movements caused the broken limb to bob, bob, bob. The harder the bob, the deeper the point jabbed into my flesh. I had no choice but to remain still—and dangle.

There I hung, one hundred and fifty pounds of boy,

on a limb that, too weak to hold me standing, yet was doing one hell of a job supporting my total dangling weight.

Spots sat beneath the tree, his big eyes staring up into mine, questioning: *What is an intelligent boy like you doing hanging there?* I stared back equally baffled, my sole satisfaction (if one can use that word) being what I had missed most about Spots—he couldn't talk. I searched my mind for a clue to the puzzle. How to get down? Each fleeting thought (one can hardly call them ideas) brought with it a slight movement of my body and the bobbing of the branch. To keep from being pierced through my back I had to clear my mind and wait—for one somebody, anybody, to pass.

Time inched by. It came to me that in my days of leisure I had not seen one person walking in the woods. Now stillness blanketed the area: every bird, every beast, every insect, had recalled that fact and so had stopped breathing, waiting for this bright boy to come up with an idea. How to unhinge himself from the broken limb of a tree.

Then I remembered Johan. He had to still be in the woods. "Spots," I said, "—Johan. Go get Johan." Spots, good dog, barked, and ran off through the trees. But the moment he had gone I felt lonely. What if he didn't come back? What if Johan misunderstood his mission and took Spots home?

Mother, I have been a child who always liked being alone. But I have never been lonely. I learned loneliness that day, dangling from a bobbing branch of a tree in the woods with Spots gone. I kept thinking of the possibility that I might be hanging there for days, weeks, forever. I imagined myself a skeleton, held up by weather-beaten strands of cloth, rattling in the wind, until, in years to come, someone attracted by the wiles of that perfect flower in full bloom looked up to discover the bones of a strange creature which once upon a time had inhabited the earth.

I wanted to cry. But to cry would shake the limb. Besides, I never have been one to give in to fear.

Then Spots came back barking and running around the tree in a frenzy. I was happy too. Nor did it matter that he had brought no one. Whatever happened, at least we had each other. And so we stayed, for hours, me hanging looking down, he sitting looking up—gazing at each other.

The sun had already begun to set, shadows had begun to thicken around the surrounding trees, when I heard a voice say, "What are you doing in that tree?" Inge. She stood beside Spots, staring up.

I hate stupid questions asked in sarcastic tones, particularly from one who obviously took delight in my discomfort. "What does it look like I'm doing?" I snapped.

"Hanging by your pants," she said, sounding smug, happy. "But then you have always been the smart one, haven't you?" She grabbed Spots by his collar and dragged him away.

Exhausted, helpless tears of pure rage formed in my eyes. I refused to call her back, hating the thought of her seeing my tears. But Spots refused to leave me. No sooner had she pulled him away than he dashed back with Inge after him. Knowing that this time she intended to get a good hold on him, I said, "Inge, are you going to leave me hanging here like this?" I hated to have to beg.

"I'm not brilliant," she said.

"But you're intelligent," I said. "And you can find a way to get me cut down."

She smiled. What an evil smile! "You're just saying that because you're up a tree," she said smugly.

"No, I'm not," I lied.

"Swear to it," she said.

"I swear. I swear. You're intelligent. You're intelligent. Please, Inge. Please," I begged. God, how I detest that girl!

"See what I can do," she said, flipping away, pleased with herself. I didn't expect to see her back.

But she did come back—with Farmer Whitley. He came bringing a ladder, which he leaned against the tree. Then, looking up, he shook his head. "Boy, what you doing up there?" When I didn't answer, he came out with a most exasperating truth. "That's a damn fool thing to do."

To have idiots stressing the obvious is maddening, especially when one is forced by circumstances to remain silent.

Farmer Whitley climbed up to me and with his machete cut my pants from the seat to my belt, then peeled the shirt from the branch, freeing me. He helped me to the ground, then said, "Boy, don't you never do a fool thing like that again."

Idiot, idiot, idiot. He had to have known that that is a once-in-a-lifetime experience.

He left us there. I stood holding on to the torn parts of my pants in the back, while Spots kept running around trying to pull the parts out of my hands. Inge stood waiting—smug, determined that I walk out ahead of her from the woods, wanting (needing) to cause me even greater embarrassment. "Carl Davis," she kept repeating, "you really do some strange things." I remained silent.

And there we stood, Inge waiting for me to go so that she could follow and see my bare behind and I equally determined that I would die first. That's the way Grandma found us.

"Junior, what in the world," she said. "I been out of my mind with worry until Farmer Whitley stopped by and told me what happened. Why ain't you come home from school?"

Whereupon bigmouthed Inge Anderson said, "School? Carl hasn't been in school but one day all week —Monday."

Grandma turned to stare down at me and I understood all that Dad meant when he talked of the "wrath of God."

"Get on home." She spoke quietly, but the weight of those words! Her very quietness was frightening. Yet I refused to move, regardless of her wrath. I had no intention of exposing my bare behind to Inge. And Inge was equally determined to squeeze me like a lemon.

Sometimes Grandma surprises me. She took in the

situation, then pushed me ahead of her and walked between us, all the while listening to Inge, who, now that she had started talking, insisted on telling all—about the composition, the teacher's reaction, the beating I had taken at Reggie's hands, which had the students still talking.

That's what happened. There's no need for hysteria or the demand that I come home. When I explained my ideas to Grandma, she insisted that she go to school to talk to my teacher. I doubt that anything will come of it. About my leaving home—I'll write, or call, to let you know my final decision.

Your Son,
Carl Davis the Third

P.S. Ma, I had already fallen asleep when Grandma awakened me. Mr. and Mrs. Anderson had come over wanting to know if I had seen Johan. How frightening. I remembered seeing him that morning, and thought about him in the clearing with those toughs. It struck me then that Spots had acted frenzied, not necessarily happy, when he had come back from looking for Johan.

I told the Andersons where he might be and we all went looking, carrying lanterns. Spots and I led the way. The car was parked in the clearing, Johan in it. He was so still. I hated his stillness. His father shook him, and when he didn't stir, Mr. Anderson got into the wreck of a car—thank goodness it had gasoline—and drove him to the hospital.

I have just come back, and seeing the book on the

dresser—*The Autobiography of Malcolm X*—which I had promised to lend him gives me a scary feeling. Why hadn't I talked to him about it before—like when I had seen him with those toughs? You see why we can't wait?

Dear Dad,

Grandma went to school today. Amazing how impressive a tiny woman can be. Grandma's back was as straight as a rod, her Sunday-go-to-church hat sat on top of her head like a warrior's helmet. Her face, calm but set, made it obvious that to deny her was to try her.

Mr. Adamson wanted to talk to her. But Grandma wanted to talk with Miss Attaway and her class. Her chatty grandchild had been called a racist, and that was a label she didn't allow.

"I have no right to disturb my classes," he said to Grandma.

"Seems to me that that class has been disturbed because of my grandson," she answered. "I aim to bring about some order."

When Miss Attaway looked up and saw us come into her room, her eyes became as hard as slate-colored marbles. Dad, I swear I have done nothing to deserve such hatred. All I do is sit in that room and try never to look at her.

"I understand that you're having some trouble with Carl junior," Grandma said, and Miss Attaway's face flamed to the roots of her hair.

"Trouble?" She shook. "Mrs. Davis, trouble is a mild word. Carl Davis is unable to communicate—with anyone outside of himself, outside of the world he lives in."

"What is it you want Junior to communicate?" Grandma asked.

"Mrs. Davis, I have a class of exceedingly bright pupils," Miss Attaway said. "Carl Davis doesn't happen to be one of them. He *thinks* he is. I spend hours trying to find ways of bringing history to life. But Carl Davis believes only in *his* interpretation of history. If we discuss British imperialism, or the expanding British Empire, Carl Davis denounces the British as colonizers and the eighteenth-century explorers, knighted by the queen, as cutthroat slave traders. When we discuss Christopher Columbus, he insists that Columbus was responsible for the destruction of the aboriginal peoples of Hispaniola— those savages." (I had said that as governor general of those islands, he should be held responsible for losing control of his European savages.) "He also blames Columbus for the introduction of slavery into this hemisphere." (Dad, I'd implied *paved* the way.)

"Carl Davis sits in class wordless. Yet when I discuss General Custer he rolls his eyes in disgust, he stares in dismay as though appalled by *my ignorance.* I asked the class to write a composition on a twentieth-century hero. Carl chose to write about a drug addict and spent an entire period reading his paper—wasting everyone's time. He refuses to study. Refuses to learn."

Whereupon Grandma rushed to my defense. "Miss Attaway, I knows Junior studies every evening far into the night."

"If he studies," Miss Attaway said with a sneer, "then I doubt your grandson's capacity to learn." Whereupon the kids giggled, clapped. Some of them cheered.

It was then that Grandma opened up on Miss Attaway. "Miss Attaway," she said, "I believe what we are talking about here are personalities. Carl junior is brilliant. His marks in his other classes, and his other schools, more than prove that. Rightly or wrongly Carl believes the things he says. If you can prove him wrong —which ain't likely—it might do him and everybody a bit of good. But Carl reads everything, from the Bible to the daily newspapers. He always has. Now, I agree that's not the easiest sort of child to get along with. He ain't normal. But dealt with he must be. The ability of being able to challenge the right and wrong of Carl Davis the Third is a mighty big challenge. But it's well worth the effort, both for you and the good of your students. He might surprise you. He might not *always* be right."

Dad, all the hostility Miss Attaway had ever felt for me, she turned on Grandma. "What do you want of me, Mrs. Davis? To spend all of my time on one child? Personalities are one thing I refuse to deal with in this room. Every matter that your grandson raises has to do with the question of race or equality.

"Look at this class, Mrs. Davis. . . ." She waved her hand around at her ninety-five-percent-white class. "Do you think we have the time to waste on issues of race?"

Grandma looked around the room. "Ain't they Americans?" she said. "Ain't being American mean facing the issue of race?" she said. "Indians, blacks, whites? And the personalities those issues formed? You say you're teaching history, Miss Attaway? Where in history was a person formed out of air? People are formed from the earth where they were born, in the air they breathed, and those what comes before them to help shape their personalities. Personalities that, as a consequence, goes to shape the lives of a people. Ain't it that the history of yesterday created the problems of today?"

Dad, Miss Attaway and Mr. Adamson stared dumbfounded. But that was nothing to the shock that raced up from the soles of my feet to my head. I turned to stone! There I stood openmouthed, listening to my grandmother!

"Miss Attaway," she said, "Mr. Adamson, and all you bright students, let me give you this one lesson in history.

"My son, Carl Davis, Jr., was born in this very town. As a boy there was no place for him to get a decent education. I took him from what was then backwoods country and brought him North. And that's history.

"Black folks been begging for a chance to learn, a chance to show themselves and the world that they, too, can develop the same knowhow as all other folks. Then in the nineteen fifties they stopped begging and started demanding that decent education—and that's history.

"In the nineteen sixties and seventies black folks walked through this land and rode through this land and sat in at counters throughout this land for the rights of all folks to be respected. And they did it peacefully. They wanted for once and for all to do away with deceit in these United States, and for all those bragging that in this country there is democracy to be speaking truth—and that's history.

"Young black folks were born with courage. It took courage to stand looking into guns, with only determination on their side. It took courage to stand up to water cannons, knowing the majority of whites were against them. It took a special kind of courage for kids, babies, to endure the attacks of vicious dogs or to sit still at counters and have lit cigarettes put out on their tender young flesh. But in the nineteen sixties and seventies they did. *That's* our history. A history of which we can all be proud. American people making American history.

"The courage of those young folks made a better place for us all to live in, to grow in, to teach in. But—there's a danger here. The danger that we forget, that teachers won't know, or care, or that the young of another generation might not benefit from that knowledge.

"No, my grandson, Carl Davis the Third, comes out of that most recent past. A lit cigarette, pushed into his father's naked flesh, pierced all the way through to his heart. That pain in his heart formed Carl Davis the Third.

"From the day he was born, it seems to me, he's been going on about history, and nobody yet has found the way to stop him. I'm here to say there ain't nothing wrong with that!"

Mr. Adamson stuttered. "Mrs. Davis, I have already said I know that Carl is advanced, but—" Grandma stopped him.

"You want to condemn him for that, Mr. Adamson?"

"No, not at all," Mr. Adamson said. "I—we think that perhaps it might be better to recommend him to another school."

"A school for the retarded, Mr. Adamson?"

"Not at all, Mrs. Davis," he said. "A school which

might be more in keeping with his—er—er—high intelligence."

Grandma pursed her lips. Her head went even higher so that she could stare down at him. I didn't have to remind her that this *was* the school for intelligent kids. She nodded. "That might be so, Mr. Adamson. Maybe Carl junior is way ahead of himself. But why rob this class of his intelligence? Every one of these young people ought to know, as their God-given right, what Junior seems to have been born knowing.

"Mr. Adamson, every link in our back is important in making our backbone. And there ain't nothing wrong in walking tall.

"Let these kids have their heroes. Let them have their sheroes. Let them have their black heroes and sheroes and their white heroes and sheroes. Let them have their George Washington and their Susan B. Anthony. Let them have their Abraham Lincoln and never let them forget their Frederick Douglass and John Brown. Let them have their Lucretia Mott and Harriet Beecher Stowe. But let them know that never a person could compare with Harriet Tubman and Rosa Parks. Let them have their Lindbergh, their Roosevelt and their Du Bois, their Martin Luther King, their Thurgood Marshall, and, yes—Let them have their Malcolm X.

"All were Americans—every last one of them, formed by this earth America and all that went before. They were formed by history and in turn made history. All did what they had to do trying to make America a better place.

"And when you discuss history, Miss Attaway,

bring out all that has made this country great. Bring out, too, the reasons why this country ain't as great as it can be.

"Yes, let these young folks have their heroes, let them know that folks ain't heroes or sheroes because of the evil they done but the good they tried to do even when they get cut down trying.

"Only then can these United States achieve true greatness. Only then will America truly deserve it. . . ."

Daddy, you never told me! Grandma is intelligent!

Your proud and grateful,
Carl Davis, Jr.

May 29

Dear Dad,

Again I thank you for having given me such an intelligent grandmother. I thought about it all day, even at school. The kids, by the way, were wonderful; most of them, both black and white (although not Inge and not Reggie), looked at me with warmth in their eyes (for the first time) and nodded and smiled. I nodded, too, and tried hard not to grin.

Tonight I told Grandma how great I thought she was —how impressive she had looked standing before the class addressing the students. (Miss Attaway didn't seem to like me any better. But you can't change them all.) "You ought to be a teacher," I told Grandma.

"I am a teacher," she said. "But only because I lived so long and have seen so many things."

"I tried to tell the students the same things you did," I said. "They never even tried to understand. With you everybody listened and enjoyed listening—I could tell."

"Junior," Grandma answered, "it's because when I spoke it was from my heart. I wanted them to benefit from my years of learning. They knew I wasn't talking just to hear myself, or to try to impress them with my— brilliance. . . ."

Dad!!!! . . .

Your humbled son,
Carl junior

Dear Mother and Dad,

On this memorial day I have something to be thankful for. Johan is going to live. I'm very happy. The Andersons have been trying to pass the word that Johan suffered a heart attack. But the gossip already leaked he had a drug overdose. Now I hear the Andersons are planning on going back home. Just like that! Here I am because you thought I smoked pot. There they go because of Johan's drug overdose.

I took Johan *The Autobiography of Malcolm X* yesterday. We talked. He told me that he heard I talked too much (bigmouthed Inge, of course). That's healthy, he said. "I want to leave here because I'm afraid to talk. When I don't agree with my friends, the way they talk about people—black people, Spanish people—I'm afraid to say so. This is not my country," he said. "I must go back home to disagree."

"Is that why you started taking drugs?" I asked.

"Drugs makes it easy not to be confused," he said. "It makes everything . . . simple."

"Why go away?" I asked. "I'm your friend. You can always talk to me."

"You're so young," he said. "My little brother, yes. Not my friend."

"I won't always be little," I said. "I'm growing. And besides, my mother said that people should never run from problems but stand and face them."

Johan laughed. "One runs out of the way of lions, even if one has a gun," he said.

When I told Grandma, she said, "Things like drugs

can be messy, especially in a town this size. Small-town folks don't mind giving a little charity," she said, "but they ain't at all charitable."

"But Mother said that people should stand and face their troubles, that it does no good to run away," I said.

"Your ma know a lot about big-city living," Grandma said. "I knows about small-town living. But after all that's said, see where she sent you, don't you?"

By the way, Mother, what about that? Oh, the agony of our contradictions!!!!

> Confused, but getting thoughtful,
> Carl junior

Dear Dad,

Of course I'm staying on here. Where else? Where can I go to have another grandmother that's so aware? Since she came to school my life has improved immeasurably. Miss Attaway doesn't like me any better, but she treats me with respect. The other students demand it. When I bring up a subject with which she might disagree, they demand a discussion in class. We might not always agree, but it's always exciting. Sometimes the discussions keep on after school is over.

Ted Thompson started speaking to me the day after. (I suppose his grandmother made him.) But Reggie Owens took a few days. When he finally stopped me in the hall he said, "Carl, you know I've always been ashamed—not of being black, but of being around white folks when they talk about blacks. I hate the way Miss Attaway—and some of the other teachers—talk down to us. They make us feel bad about slavery and about always causing trouble—know what I mean?

"I always wanted to be considered just an American," he said. "And they never let me. But the way your grandmother explained things, I'm ashamed of being ashamed."

I wanted to be gracious, but let's face it, Dad, it's hard to forgive someone who beat the hell out of you. "If you had listened carefully to what I had to say instead of beating on me, you might have come to that conclusion sooner."

"I'm ashamed of that too," he said. "Not of beating on you but of what I said to Mr. Adamson."

"I hadn't done anything for you to beat on me," I answered.

"You were always acting as though you thought you were so much better than anyone else," he said.

I started to say that I had not been acting better, just brighter. But I had heard what Grandma said, about speaking from her heart. I'd heard it deeply. So I said, "If that's the way I sounded, it wasn't my intention. I suppose *I was afraid* of being talked down to. I could never accept that." (How's that for being the diplomat, Dad?)

Reggie nodded, understanding my fears. I think we're going to be friends. But then, I knew from the first he was an intelligent boy.

Your grateful son,
Carl junior

Dear Dad,

Grandma and Deacon Johnson were sitting out on the porch discussing poor Johan, so I listened. I didn't mean to eavesdrop. But I heard Deacon Johnson say, "Sure we expect to find drugs in the big city. But right here in our own backyard?"

Grandma said, "What to do? Wherever you find drugs it's deadweight—almost more than the human soul can bear. I tell you, Deacon," she said, "if those freedom fighters hadn't kept things moving, if Malcolm X hadn't been on the scene preaching against drugs, it would have been a dead Mary Jo Davis you would have been thinking about.

"Yes, sir, them freedom rides took up Carl's energies and Malcolm X cleared out his mind, or I do declare, the both of us would have been long dead. As it is, here he is practically an old man and got to finish what he had so long started. Look at them years it took out of his life."

Deacon Johnson agreed. "Them years don't be waiting around, sister. If you don't be moving right along with 'em, they just overtake you, roll right over you, and keeps right on going. . . ."

Dad, I listened, I heard. Then two minutes later I understood!!!

You? My Dad? Into drugs!!! In all of our years of honesty, of openness, why have you never told me? Of all the confusing moments in my life this moment must be the most dense. I cannot think. I can only repeat again and again—my Dad, the doctor I always bragged about—a drug addict! My confusion thickens.

Carl junior

Dear Dad,

I feel only tenderness toward Grandma. When I think of how she must have suffered because of you. Still, she doesn't hold it against you. I do. I feel I must make it up to her. I have decided to devote my entire life to her—to live down here, with her, in the great outdoors.

As a son I have been disillusioned. It maddens me to think of all the things I haven't known about you. I think of the days, weeks, months, years, tipping around that apartment in consideration of you, of mother— helping you both to get through your studies. I ran to you with all my little confidences. The faith I had in you! The thoughts I thought we shared. While all the time you were keeping things, a lifetime of things, from me.

I never want to tip around a house again, or turn down my radio or stereo. I never want to whisper when I have a desire to talk loud, or hum, or sing, or shout. What an abnormal childhood I have had. How deprived. Thank God, that's over. I never want to have to live through such misery again!!!

Your son,
Carl junior

Dear Mother,

Why must you get so hysterical every time you call? It's most upsetting. Yes, I miss you and Dad. I forgive you your lack of faith in me. I understand all. But I don't want to come home.

Grandma is a truly great woman. After I hung up the phone she wanted to know why I was so hard on my parents. "Me? Hard? I'm the one betrayed, remember?" I told her.

Then I told her that I had heard her conversation with the deacon about my father having been an addict. "Junior," she said, "how you got Malcolm X as your hero? How you understand so much about Johan, and you wants to turn your back against your father, who did nothing but love you?

"I love your father," she said. "He's a wonderful man. He had a big future promised to him because his father worked for it. He made a detour but pulled his own self up and went at it again. I'm proud of my son. And I'm proud and grateful of your mother too.

"That drug is a force. A mighty powerful force that can destroy. I ran from it. Your mother could have too. But she stuck it out *with him*, worked with him until he got it together.

"Now they're on their way. A bit old. He's well into his forties and she's pushing the hell out of forty-five— one side or the other, quiet as that's kept. But they're together."

"Why didn't they ever tell me?" I said. "I'm understanding."

"Junior," Grandma said, "folks live some of the best and most important part of their lives long before their children happen along. They have many problems. Some they resolve and decide to forget. That's got to be their right."

"They didn't forget," I said. "When they thought I might be on drugs, instead of trusting me, giving me a hearing, they put me on a train."

"Got nothing to do with trust," Grandma said. "It's got to do with fear."

"Fear? Because I took one puff on a joint?"

"Fear is nature's way of saving lives, Junior. Your folks was scared to death that if they discussed it with you, you might want to outdo your daddy. Fathers are the role models for sons. They were afraid that if they told you their reasoning, the way you always must win out in an argument—you might just talk them out of doing what they thought they had to do.

"Junior, your grandpa worked hard to send your daddy through school. It took all the money he ever made in his life, and more, to get away from this town and up to that big city so your daddy could get to a decent school. In the city he had to take jobs and in-between jobs, and I had to take jobs and in-between jobs, to afford to live. Kept him from being home so that father and son hardly knew one another. It took all of my free time—and strength—to rear your daddy. Still he took to the streets.

"We were poor," Grandma said. "Black folks are poor folks, Junior—in this country, in this world. Ain't that what you're always running out of your mouth about? Our heroes. Our heroes are poor heroes. Those handful of movie stars and rock stars and ballplayers on TV—they're dreams, Junior. Our dreams. Poor folks kept the Revolution going, Junior. Poor folks will keep it going. It was that sixties and seventies revolution that got your daddy to quit nodding that big head of his on street corners and get it back in the books.

"By that time his pa was long dead—misery of the heart, don't you know. And I had put myself on a train and gained distance from that big evil city.

"I blamed your granddad for leaving our little home. But he had seen this place as a dead end for Carl junior. He believed in his son. When I came back I saw the city as dead end for my only child. I saw him as dead! The one thing I had was this house I had to come back to.

"Now look at your daddy. A big doctor in a position to help poor folks. I sure ain't earned the right to be righteous, Junior. Neither have you."

"All I'm saying, Grandma," I told her, "is that they ought to have discussed everything with me."

"They still got time. You're alive, ain't you?" she said.

"Junior, every generation needs something to withstand the pressures of their times. It started with man wanting to feel he's better than all other animals. He wrote the Bible and still needed wine. The harder the pressure, the stronger the brew. And this is a pressure-cooker time, wouldn't you say, bright boy?"

So I understand—and forgive—your lack of faith in me, Mother. But I don't want to go home.

> Your humble son,
> Carl

P.S. I said to Grandma I ought to have talked to her first before I got so hurt. She said, "Cakes that take their own time to rise generally comes out better."

What a magnificent lady. I love her and shall never leave her. She is so fragile, so dainty, and so intelligent. Besides, she's getting old. I love her very much. I love you too. . . .

> C.D.

Dear Folks,

I went to see the Andersons. They're packed to leave. When I got to their house, the parents had gone to the hospital to get Johan. Yesterday was our last day of school. When I walked up, Inge was alone on the front steps. When she saw me coming, she called to Spots and, to prevent him from running to me, held him by his collar. She's the one person in class who has remained hostile.

"What do you want here?" she asked.

I had come to see Spots and Johan and to say good-bye to her and to her parents. But I told her I had come to talk to her parents.

"What about?" she asked. "Are you afraid that we'll leave the country and they'll never know what a big mouth you have? Don't worry. I told them."

I had come with all intentions of being charming—gracious, if you will. I wanted, because it was our last meeting, to end on a pleasant note. I also wanted, if I had the occasion, to confide in her parents, to tell them about Dad, add his name to Malcolm's as great men who had conquered drugs. I had even convinced myself that I might have been to blame for the poor relationship between Inge and me—until I spoke to her.

"I don't think you're that smart," she said. "If you were, why did it take so long for you to get the students to like you?" She had a point which I might have conceded had her attitude been different. (I'm cultivating simplicity of manner—it makes Grandma happy.) Reggie and I are friends. He, and sometimes Ted, misses the school bus so that we can stay together and discuss problems concerning us as we sit fishing on the shore of the lake. Then he has to take the city bus back to town.

So I said to Inge, "Do you know you're the one person in the entire class who has absolutely no saving grace?"

"At least I'm not so stupid that I hang from trees by the seat of my pants and beg," she said.

Mother, Dad, I am trying to appear like a normal child. But I refuse to tolerate anyone who so thoroughly enjoys washing my face in my shame. Still, I fought for control.

"What month were you born, Inge?" I asked.

"What do you care?" she answered.

"I have the gift of being able to read horoscopes," I lied, knowing how females are addicted to astrology. "Don't you want to know your future before you leave?"

"I was born in February. What is my fortune?" she asked in the way of those anxious to get something free.

So I told her. "You are short, squat, and misshapen. You shall always be short, squat, and misshapen. And as you grow older you shall be ugly."

"And you are a sexist," she screamed at me. "That's why you say those things to me. You're a twisted-minded sexist."

I walked out of the yard. But her words really hurt. It seemed that she had had the last word. And from what I had said to her—they sounded true.

Carl

Dear Mom, Dad,

I shall be coming home after all. It is a most unhappy thought. I am becoming accustomed to my school and have been looking forward to next year when I will freely mingle with boys and girls—one of those developing TE. Reggie and I talk about this. (My simple manner really works.) We talk about the good times we intend to have and we are both looking forward to how our friendship will develop.

I no longer miss your asphalt jungle with its square little parks where poor animals merely survive (you ought to see the woods now, bursting green and alive with animals), but . . .

Today, I came home and, seeing Deacon Johnson's car parked out front, went around the back. Walking through to the front of the house I saw Grandma and Deacon Johnson on the front porch. Mom, Dad, Deacon Johnson was kissing Grandma!!!!

That old man! I waited, expecting her to push those creaky bones back into the rocking chair. She didn't. Then he said, "Mary Jo, this kissing here and kissing there and sneaking and jumping when we hear a sound is for young folks, not old folks like us. How long's this damn foolishness going to keep on?"

And Grandma said, "What to do, Deacon? So long as Junior feels like staying on here, here's where he'll stay. Can you imagine if I sent him back? What if something happened to him up there?"

"Something like what?" Deacon Johnson said. "He ain't dumb enough to stand in the street for no car to hit him. Nobody gonna kidnap him. Any sucker fool enough to try will pay his folks to take him back soon's he gits to talking. Be telling all 'bout the history of kidnapping."

Grandma laughed. Dad, Mom, the deacon was talking about me and Grandma laughed! Then she said, "Things'll work out, Deacon. Junior is growing fast. Ain't you noticed? He goes around the house asking instead of telling. And he ain't broken a thing for the longest time."

"What's left to break?" old Deacon asked. Then he said, "Tell you one thing, Mary Jo, if we sit around waiting for things to work out, time would have done rolled over me. All will be left are these old bones for you to bury."

Grandma laughed again. "You know what I always did love about you, Deacon—is your sense of humor."

Sense of humor! Is that all Grandma wants? To watch an old man eat and sleep so she can laugh herself to death!!!

I'm very unhappy about this development (having to go back to the city when I want to be staying in the country—and leaving Grandma sitting around laughing, just waiting to bury old bones). . . . After I finish this letter I shall go down to the lake to fish—and think.

Your son,
Carl

P.S. Mom, Dad, no sooner did I get down to the lake than Inge came with Spots. Her family had gone over to our house, and not finding me there, she came looking for me.

"How is Johan?" I asked.

"Better," she said. "We're leaving today. My father's work here is done. We're going home."

"I guess Johan will be happy to get back," I said.

"So will I," Inge said. "I'm unhappy in your country. I have no real friends."

But everybody likes her—or seems to. Yet thinking back, it suddenly occurred to me that Inge has always been alone—except for around the school. I thought of Johan, remembering his unhappiness. I had never felt that quality of loneliness in her.

"The girls like me all right," she said, "because I'm from Europe. They like to ask me questions about Europe. But they don't really like to be with me. I'm strange to them—different."

She had always seemed strange to me. Now her saying it put me in the same category with all the rest. The times we might have been friends I had not been too open—which made me feel like an ordinary American. "Anyway, back in Sweden," she said, "I have real friends. I have grandparents. . . ."

"Yes, grandparents are important," I agreed. "I know."

But Inge misinterprets everything I say. She got angry. "Oh, you always know."

"It does seem that way, doesn't it?" I spoke gently, but she didn't hear—or wasn't used to my new manner.

"Your grandmother is a wonderful lady but you're horrible," she said.

"And you are still fat and squat and funny-looking," I said.

"And you're still a sexist," she said. "I don't know why Spots likes you more than he likes me."

"Spots is a bright dog," I said. "He hates retards."

After all, *she* had called *me* retarded, remember? And she had called me sexist. I'm neither. Still, when tears stood out in her eyes, I felt guilty and had to admit that I would never have described her shape that way if she had been a boy. So I apologized.

"I'm sorry, Inge," I said. "I really didn't mean those things." (Mom, Dad, your son actually apologized.) "You're not going to be short and fat and squat—no more than I." (I certainly hope not!!!) "You're going to be tall, taller than your mother, and more beautiful." (I always have believed that.)

Her eyes cleared, her face brightened. "Do you really think so?" she asked.

"I know so. It's in your stars," I said. "You're the prettiest girl in class," I said. "As a matter of fact you're the prettiest girl in the whole school." (I told you she was, didn't I? Knowing me, I assume you read between the lines.)

"Why didn't you ever tell me?" she wanted to know.

"Because I'm shy," I said.

"You?" She didn't believe it. (Neither did I.) But a burning started from the soles of my feet and rushed through to my head. I wanted to disappear after that confession. Ma, I have never blushed over a girl before! (Dad, you think that that might be the start of TE????)

112

"I hope that doesn't make you think I'm even more sexist," I said.

"No, that makes you the most interesting boy in class, in the entire school—as well as the most intelligent."

"You never told me you thought that," I said.

"I told my mother and my father and my brother. I told them, he is so intelligent and so sexist, he's obnoxious."

"I like you, too, Inge Anderson," I said, relieved to be free of my new indictment. (I couldn't be a sexist, could I, Mother? After all, you are and have been my role model since I can remember.)

Inge's eyes grew bigger and brighter. Then she said, "I like you, too, Carl Davis the Third. And I am happy to be leaving my dog, Spots, with you."

She pushed Spots's leash into my hand! Mom, Dad, I wanted to die of happiness!

Spots belongs to me! I'm bringing him home! You'll love him. Never in your life have you seen a dog so devoted, so intelligent. How lucky I am. To be seeing my mother, my father, my friend Selena, soon, and to have my very own dog, and to be able to visit Grandma whenever I wish. And, too, I have to start planning seriously for my first trip abroad—to Sweden. (I promised Inge.) My life just keeps opening and opening and opening. What a wonderful life. . . .

> Your loving son and proud owner of Spots,
> Carl

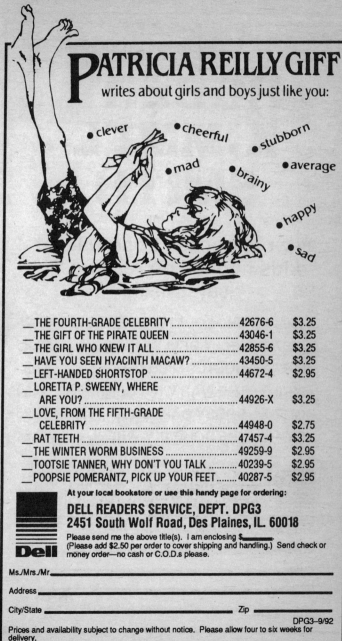